LOVE AND THE SINGLE DAD

SUSAN CROSBY

SPECIAL EDITION

Published by Silhouette Books

America's Publisher of Contemporary Romance

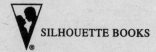

SILHOUETTE BOOKS

Recycling programs
for this product may
not exist in your area.

ISBN-13: 978-0-373-65501-4

LOVE AND THE SINGLE DAD

Copyright © 2010 by Susan Bova Crosby

All rights reserved. Except for use in any review, the reproduction
or utilization of this work in whole or in part in any form by any
electronic, mechanical or other means, now known or hereafter
invented, including xerography, photocopying and recording, or in
any information storage or retrieval system, is forbidden without
the written permission of the editorial office, Silhouette Books,
233 Broadway, New York, NY 10279 U.S.A.

This is a work of fiction. Names, characters, places and incidents are
either the product of the author's imagination or are used fictitiously, and
any resemblance to actual persons, living or dead, business establishments,
events or locales is entirely coincidental.

This edition published by arrangement with Harlequin Books S.A.

® and TM are trademarks of Harlequin Books S.A., used under license.
Trademarks indicated with ® are registered in the United States Patent
and Trademark Office, the Canadian Trade Marks Office and in other
countries.

Visit Silhouette Books at www.eHarlequin.com

Printed in U.S.A.

Books by Susan Crosby

Silhouette Special Edition

*The Bachelor's Stand-In Wife #1912
**The Rancher's Surprise Marriage #1922
*The Single Dad's Virgin Wife #1930
*The Millionaire's Christmas Wife #1936
††The Pregnant Bride Wore White #1995
††Love and the Single Dad #2019

Silhouette Desire

†Christmas Bonus, Strings Attached #1554
†Private Indiscretions #1570
†Hot Contact #1590
†Rules of Attraction #1647
†Heart of the Raven #1653
†Secrets of Paternity #1659
The Forbidden Twin #1717
Forced to the Altar #1733
Bound by the Baby #1797

*Wives for Hire
††The McCoys of Chance City
**Back in Business
†Behind Closed Doors

SUSAN CROSBY

believes in the value of setting goals, but also in the magic of making wishes, which often do come true—as long as she works hard enough. Along life's journey she's done a lot of the usual things—married, had children, attended college a little later than the average coed and earned a B.A. in English. Then she dove off the deep end into a full-time writing career, a wish come true.

Susan enjoys writing about people who take a chance on love, sometimes against all odds. She loves warm, strong heroes, and good-hearted, self-reliant heroines, and she will always believe in happily ever after.

More can be learned about her at www.susancrosby.com.

To Patti Rueb with gratitude for your ego-boosting notes, and your friendship.

And Robin Burcell, yet again. You know why.

"Not so bad, hmm?" he asked.

She didn't answer. Couldn't answer. Her heart was lodged in her throat. Every nerve ending did pirouettes throughout her body. But she was also aware that a lot of people were watching them. So while she wanted to lean against him and use the excuse of dancing to snuggle close, she pulled back a little, putting some space between them, and stumbling over his feet at the same time.

He laughed, low and sexy. "You're so obvious."

She met his teasing gaze. "About what?"

"About wanting me. You'll even trip just to get closer."

"In your dreams."

"Oh, yeah. Dreams for sure," he whispered into her ear. "Hot ones. Detailed ones."

Dear Reader,

It's probably obvious to say that I've never created a hero I didn't totally, absolutely adore. Why would I write any other kind of man? They've all shared certain characteristics: honesty, loyalty, kindness, intelligence, wit. Who doesn't want all that in a hero—or a human being, for that matter?

But a fictional hero needs to be more than what's expected. He's generally a man who accepts huge challenges and takes the necessary risks to meet them. He needs drive and guts above and beyond the average.

Donovan McCoy is such a hero. He's worked hard and achieved success professionally, but where has that gotten him personally? Then at the peak of his career, Donovan discovers he's a father. Now what? What constitutes success now? How does he balance work and home? It's an issue that many parents battle, whether married or single.

I hope you enjoy Donovan's journey to discovering what's really important in life, and how he goes about achieving it.

Susan

Chapter One

Donovan McCoy tossed his duffel bag into his rented SUV, then ran a mental checklist of his briefcase contents—e-ticket, passport, voice recorder, laptop, cell phone. Chargers? He needed to double-check that he'd gathered all of them. An hour ago he'd added a stack of Internet research to pore over during the flights. Last night he'd said goodbye to his family at a farewell barbecue, thirty-two goodbyes, to be precise, from his eighty-nine-year-old grandmother to his two-month-old niece.

The McCoy clan knew how to throw a party.

Donovan shut the car door with more force than necessary. He was on edge this morning. Not wanting to analyze why, he strode back up the walkway to his brother's house. A car pulled up, a shiny red Miata, the convertible top down to take advantage of the warm July day.

"I hear you're leaving," the driver called out.

Laura Bannister. He'd managed to stay in town for two months without any one-on-one conversations with her. Intentionally. Their long-ago-but-brief history amounted to a single event when she was a freshman in high school and he was a senior. She'd made him an offer he'd been smart enough to refuse, but had regretted his decision ever since. Even though fifteen years had gone by, the memory hadn't faded.

Donovan ambled over to her car, studying her as he went. Her hair was down, rare for her, and wind-tossed, even rarer. He'd never seen her looking anything but perfect—sedate, elegant and neat. Her wild look wasn't the image he wanted stuck in his head from now on, not this accessible, sexily messy woman with the ash-blond flyaway hair, her trendy sunglasses hiding eyes he recalled were hazel and always direct.

He rested an arm on the top of her windshield, checked out her white shorts and pink tank top. Her nickname around town was "The Body."

"It's Tuesday and you're not working, Laura?"

"I'm playing hooky."

"Hell froze over? Pigs flew?"

She gave him that look, her lawyer look, the one that set a person in his place. He'd always found it sexy.

"So, where are you headed this time?" she asked.

"I'm going to mosey down Mexico way. Do a follow-up on the article I did last month for *NewsView*."

"Is it risky?"

"Guess I'll find out."

She shoved her sunglasses up into her hair and squinted against the sun. "Your family loved having you home for so long."

"I'm sure Joe'll be glad to have his house to himself again." His brother hadn't said anything, but Donovan figured he'd overstayed. Which might be a clue that he shouldn't wait another twelve years to take a vacation and be in such need for time off.

"You're probably right," Laura said. "I've lived alone for so long, I'm not sure I could ever adapt to sharing space with someone."

"You and me both." He was glad they hadn't had this conversation anytime in the past two months. He didn't want to discover anything in common with her. She was five foot eight, shapely, stunning and smart— a deadly combination, the kind of woman he went for. And a complication he didn't want….

Because she was from here, Chance City, his hometown, the place he'd left behind without regrets the day after high-school graduation fifteen years ago.

"I should let you get on the road." Laura settled her sunglasses back in place and grabbed the gearshift knob.

He tapped the windshield to get her attention.

"What does Laura Bannister, ex-beauty queen and attorney-at-law, do when she plays hooky?"

"Just that—I play. It's a day of self-indulgence. I had a massage, and now I'm going to go home, take a swim, then stretch out on a lounge chair and read something other than case files."

An image flashed in his mind, based on an old e-mail from his brother Jake. "I heard about the bikini you wore at a Labor Day party last year."

"Did you?" Her mouth curved into the sexiest smile he'd ever seen, her lips glossy and pale pink. "Well, I don't bother with a swimsuit at home. Too confining. Bye, Donovan. Be safe."

He decided not to stare after her like a randy teenager as she drove off, although he felt like one, so he went inside to make a final check of the house. From the dining-room table he picked up a copy of a photo his nephew had taken of the whole family at the barbecue last night. The teenager had rushed home and printed copies for everyone, had even put Donovan's in a travel frame, now tucked away in his duffel. People always had a hard time believing he had five sisters, two brothers and seventeen nieces and nephews. Now he had proof to show.

It'd been a good couple of months, especially spending time with his brothers. Jake, older by four years, had gone fishing with him, like the old days. Joe, younger by three years and the baby of the family, had become a man—probably long ago, but Donovan had finally spent enough time with Joe to recognize his maturity.

And his loneliness. But that was for Joe to figure out.

With nothing left to do, Donovan poured himself a to-go cup of coffee, checked his briefcase for the chargers, then headed out. The phone rang. He debated whether to let it go to Joe's answering machine. Most people called his cell phone, so it was probably a telemarketer.

But because Donovan was in stall mode, he picked up the phone.

"Oh, good, I caught you in time. This is Honey." The forthright woman owned the Take a Lode Off Diner, the local gathering place where truth and gossip mingled freely, but he couldn't hear the usual diner noise in the background.

"I'm headed to the airport right now, Honey. What's up?"

"There's a woman here at the Lode looking for you."

"Who?"

"Didn't catch her first name. Blond. British. Last name sounded like Bogart, maybe?"

"Bogard," he corrected automatically. Anne Bogard. What the hell was she doing here, especially after all these years without contact?

"Donovan? Are you there?"

"Yeah." Now what? "What did you tell her?"

"That I would see if you'd left town yet."

He should trust his instincts and ask Honey to say

she hadn't caught him. But curiosity—and something even stronger—changed his mind. "Send her here to Joe's, please, Honey."

"Will do."

Donovan shoved his hands in his pockets, memories assaulting him. He and Anne had ended their relationship over five years ago. They'd both been covering the war in Afghanistan, both freelance photojournalists working as close to the front lines as possible. It was where he'd made his name, garnering credibility and a few awards, opening up his world, personally and professionally.

The breakup with Anne had been bitter, neither of them willing to compromise their blossoming careers for a personal relationship. He'd seen her name on a byline now and then, but her career hadn't gone the same way as his. He took every chance in the book. She played it safe, for several years writing character pieces, and articles about members of royalty from all over Europe, but nothing at all lately, not that he'd seen. A far cry from their time dodging missiles.

He was over her. Had been over her for a long time. Yet his heart pounded when he saw a dark blue sedan park in front of the house. Should he wait for her to knock? She knew he was home and waiting for her, so it hardly made sense to stay inside.

He opened the front door, stepped out.

Her car door swung open—

Not Anne. It was Millie, Anne's mother. She raised her hand, gave a tentative wave.

Dread curled inside Donovan, burning hot. If Millie had come all the way from Great Britain to see him, the news couldn't be good.

On autopilot, he kept moving down the walkway as she came around the front of the car.

"Hello, Millie," he said, questions rushing through his mind.

"Donovan. You're looking well."

She hugged him, sending all that red-hot dread skittering through him. She wasn't a hugger. It had taken him a while to get used to, because his mother hugged everyone, long and hard.

He waited, mind whirling, pulse racing, heart thundering.

"I'll tell you straight out, then," she said. "Anne died last month."

His world tilted. "What happened?"

"Lymphoma. She fought it for a long time."

Shock hit him, followed immediately by grief. She'd been so beautiful, so vital. "I'm very sorry, Millie. She was an incredible woman."

"Yes, she was." She paused. "I suppose you're wondering why I've come."

He nodded, especially since he was rarely here, had never given out this address as his.

She looked ready to speak, then clamped her mouth shut. "I'll just show you, then."

She opened the back door of the car and held out

her hand. A child emerged. A boy. With black hair and blue eyes.

Like me, Donovan thought, as Millie confirmed it out loud.

"This is your son, Ethan."

Chapter Two

Donovan brought Millie a mug of tea and Ethan a glass of milk, then set a plate of his mother's home-made chocolate chip cookies on the coffee table.

Ethan. His son. A son he'd been denied for almost five years.

Why? What possible reason could Anne have had to keep his own son from him?

"Had enough time to get used to it?" Millie asked Donovan as he joined her on the couch. Ethan played quietly with race cars from Joe's toy cupboard, but looked up now and then at Donovan, his gaze serious. So far, the boy hadn't said a word.

No, Donovan hadn't had enough time yet, but he

needed answers. He leaned toward Millie. "Does he talk?"

"Oh, yes. He's a regular chatterbox, that one. He's had a long day, that's all. Give him a little time, and he'll be right as rain." She sipped her tea. "Lovely, thanks."

"Don't you think we should discuss this privately, Millie?"

"Perhaps you should read the paperwork first." She passed him a portfolio a couple of inches thick, filled with folders and envelopes. "I'd start at the top. It'll make more sense that way."

Because he needed to know the big picture before the details, he sifted through the folders and envelopes to determine the contents. He found legal documents—Anne's trust, Ethan's birth certificate with Donovan's name listed as father, Anne's birth certificate. One envelope held a journal, the first entry being the day she learned she was pregnant. The final entry on Mother's Day, two months ago. Another envelope contained pieces of Ethan's artwork and crafts, from first scribbles to more complex collages.

"There's more," Millie said. "In my suitcase."

Ethan had put away the race cars and was now building a tower with interlocking plastic squares. His mouth was set in concentration, a dab of chocolate at one corner.

Finally Donovan went back to the beginning and opened the first envelope in the stack, a handwritten letter from Anne. He closed his eyes for a moment, then began to read.

Dear Donovan,

I know you will never forgive me for not telling you I was pregnant, and then keeping Ethan from you. I didn't want a part-time father for my son, especially a father who accepted all dares and took all risks, one who journeyed far and wide to tell the truth to the world.

I'd wanted the same kind of career for myself, as you know, but I gave that up to become a full-time parent, something you wouldn't have done. I wanted Ethan to have stability, so I chose to raise him myself. Consistency is critical for a child.

As he got older I changed my mind, mostly because my mother begged me over and over. So, I was going to involve you, I promise you that, but then I was diagnosed with lymphoma. It changed everything. I needed to make memories with my son so that he would remember me. I couldn't do that and share him with you at the same time. My mother has photo albums for you, and we shot lots of videos.

Please keep my memory alive for him. And please stay in touch with my mother so that Ethan will continue to know her. You have a large family, which will be a boon for him, particularly while you're on assignment, but Mum needs to be part of that family, too.

Finally, I hope you prove me wrong, that I've worried for no reason. I almost asked my mother to keep Ethan, maintaining the consistency he needs, because I'm afraid you'll let someone else in your family raise him. I know how much your career matters. Your search for truth and justice has driven you to places most nonmilitary people never go. I've seen your scars, both physical and emotional. It's a young man's game, and you're still young. I don't see you giving it up like I did. But Ethan has already lost me. I hope you keep that in mind while deciding what to do next.

Thank you for the gift of my son. He made my life worthwhile.

We were both too selfish, Donovan.

Anne

Donovan folded up the paper and slipped it back into the envelope. Selfish? About what, his career? That was true. He wouldn't have been selfish about his son, however. She hadn't given him a chance to show that.

She'd been the selfish one. And she was right—he would never forgive her for that.

"Questions?" Millie asked.

He nodded. "But I want to read everything thoroughly first. You're not going to rush off, are you? I need to talk to a lawyer. You might be needed."

"I wouldn't drop him off and leave. He needs transition time. He's become quite attached to me, as you can imagine."

An anchor in a swirling sea. Yes, he could imagine any child needing that. "How would you feel about staying with my mother? I can get you a motel room, if you'd rather, but—"

"In for a penny, in for a pound," she said cheerfully.

He smiled for the first time since she'd driven up. "Exactly."

"I'd like to know the people my lad will be spending his life with, so a couple of days would be grand. If you're quite sure your mum won't mind."

"If I took you to a motel, she'd just drive up and get you, so, yes, I'm sure she won't mind. I'll stay at Mom's, too. This is my brother Joe's home. I don't have a house here in town." He gestured toward the stack of paperwork. "His birth certificate says he was born in Maine."

"Anne didn't plan it that way. She was there on a job interview to teach at the university since her writing wasn't going to pay the bills entirely, but she went into labor. He was a month premature."

"I thought women couldn't fly in their last trimester." Millie cocked her head.

"I've got five sisters. I hear things," he said, trying to make light of it. But it was typical of Anne that she'd taken such a risk. She'd probably convinced some doctor to give his approval.

"Well, you know Anne," Millie said, echoing his thoughts. "She ended up getting the job and staying on."

"Why would she choose Maine, of all places?"

"She said it was because you wouldn't think to look for her there."

That confused him. "With very little digging, I could've found her. I saw her byline occasionally. I could've contacted her publisher."

"But you never did, did you? Maybe she wanted you to find her, I don't know. Why didn't you come looking for her?"

"Because it was over."

"It didn't occur to you to find out if she was pregnant after you split up? You'd been together quite a while."

Six months. Long enough to have fallen hard for her, but not long enough for her to feel the same. "It never would've occurred to me that she wouldn't contact me to say she was pregnant." *Selfish.* He had a feeling that word was going to come up a lot.

He focused on Millie then. "My mom and grandmother drove to Sacramento this morning, but they'll be back in a few hours. Would you mind staying here while I go talk to my lawyer? I'll let my brother know, so he doesn't come home to find you without warning."

"That would be all right."

He walked over to where Ethan was playing, his tower a couple of feet tall and wobbly. His child, and he hadn't even touched him.

Donovan laid a hand on Ethan's shoulder. The boy jerked back a little, and Donovan quickly released him.

"I'm your father."

Ethan nodded.

Love rushed through Donovan, a powerful need to protect this sad, worried child of his. "I'd like to give you a hug," he said, trying to keep his voice steady.

Ethan looked at Millie, who smiled and nodded. "Go on, then, love. It's okay."

Still Ethan hesitated.

"Maybe later," Donovan said, disappointed but understanding. "I have to go somewhere for a little while, but I'll be back. I promise I'll be back. If you want to rest, there are two bedrooms. You can use either one. Or you can just keep playing."

"I'll play, thanks. These toys are wicked fun."

Donovan laughed at the New England term, although said with a slight British inflection. "Yes, your uncle Joe has a wicked-good toy cupboard."

He wrote down his cell phone number and gave it to Millie; then he escaped.

Escaped. There was no other word for it, he thought, as he got into the car he was supposed to return today. He needed to cancel his flight, too. He did that as he drove, then called Joe but only got his voice mail.

"Hey, it's me. Listen, I haven't left town. Something came up. Give me a call as soon as you get this. Thanks."

He pulled up in front of Laura Bannister's house. Knowing she was probably in her backyard sunbathing—without a confining bikini—gave him a little bit of mental distraction from thinking about how his life had just been turned upside down and then spun on its axis.

Because everything had changed. Everything.

Donovan sat in his car, trying to right himself. The spinning slowed, as did his heart rate. He'd been trapped by enemy fire more than once, and this felt just as terrifying.

He wished he had Laura's home number. He could get her office number, but that wouldn't help. So he walked to the blue-painted front door and rang the bell. After a few seconds, he tried again. One more time.

The door opened. She must have looked through the peephole because she didn't show surprise. Her face was pink from the sun. Her skin gleamed with sunscreen and sweat. She wore a pink-flowered shift with skimpy straps over bare shoulders, which meant she really had been sunbathing in the nude. Too bad he didn't have the time or inclination to let his imagination take that picture and run with it.

"Donovan?"

He said the words out loud for the first time. "I have a son."

Chapter Three

Laura gauged the tension in Donovan's body, the restrained emotion in his eyes, and invited him in.

"Grab something cold from the refrigerator," she said, gesturing toward the kitchen. "I need to change."

He headed that way. She rushed into her bedroom, pulled on a pair of cropped pants and a blouse, twisted her hair up with a big clip and then grabbed a legal pad and pen.

From the living room, she spotted him outdoors, a bottle of water hanging loosely in one hand, the portfolio he'd brought in the other. He moved closer to her pool, staring into it. Although not large, it was pretty, and set within a small forest for privacy. Peace and quiet reigned, a paradise of her own creation.

Laura didn't join him right away but studied the tall, ruggedly handsome man. She'd tried to avoid him the whole time he was home, but he kept popping up everywhere she went—parties, picnics, even at the diner when she dropped in for lunch or coffee. They were polite to each other, but never engaged in conversation, not just the two of them alone, anyway. It'd been especially hard this trip, because he usually came home for only a few days, and then was gone again.

And she'd never known a man who intrigued her more or whom she needed to steer clear of more.

She couldn't think about that now, or that time in high school, either. She opened the glass doors and joined him. "Do you want to stay out here or go inside?" she asked.

"You choose."

"Inside, then. It's cooler."

"I'm sorry I interrupted your day of self-indulgence," he said, coming back to life a little.

"Oh, well. It was self-indulgent of me, anyway."

He barely smiled. "I think I have need of a lawyer."

They both sat. He took an overstuffed chair. She perched on the sofa so that the coffee table would be handy for paperwork. "And since I'm the only family-law attorney in town, you settled for me?"

"If I didn't think you were the best, here or anywhere, I wouldn't have come to you."

Right answer. He seemed a little more relaxed finally,

so she opened up the discussion to business. "Okay. So…you have a son?"

"Ethan. He'll be five in a month."

Laura listened to his story and sifted through the documents.

"What happens?" he asked. "Do I adopt him?"

"No need. You're listed as his father. But, Donovan, are you sure he's yours? We should verify."

"There's a picture on Mom's photo wall—my first day in kindergarten. It could be Ethan. And the timing is right. I don't question his paternity."

His cell phone rang. "I'm sorry, Laura. I need to warn Joe that they're at his house."

While Donovan explained the situation to his brother, Laura reread Anne's trust documents, but what she really wanted to read was her journal. Too bad there wasn't a legal reason for that. She thumbed an envelope that he said contained a personal letter from Anne.

Donovan noticed. He put his hand over the phone. "Go ahead."

He'd loved her, that much Laura had figured out from the way he talked about her. He was angry and hurt, too, but he'd loved her. He was also a family man, and the fact that he hadn't known about his son all this time had to be devastating. It didn't matter that he'd left his home and family so many years ago. They were still the most important people in his life.

And a son? She didn't know how much of a change

he would've made in his career decisions, but he certainly would've done *something*.

Anne implied in her letter that he would let his family raise the boy, only visiting now and then. Laura wasn't so sure about that. She also didn't know how many options he had. He was at the top of his game. How could he make a huge change at this point in his career without risking it entirely?

"Sorry," Donovan said, slipping his phone into his pocket.

"How did Joe react?"

His mouth tightened. "I can't repeat his words to a lady—which is not the word he used to describe Anne."

Brother protective of brother. Family ties. Laura's experience with them were minimal. Her parents had divorced when she was a baby, and her mother hadn't remarried. As a family-law attorney, however, she saw all kinds of familial relationships and had come to appreciate what she had with her mother.

"You probably heard me tell him to get it out of his system right now," Donovan continued. "I won't tolerate any bad-mouthing. She's my son's mother. That's all that matters."

"That's commendable of you."

"I'm not as uncivilized as some people think."

She raised her brows. "You've changed overnight?"

After a moment he laughed. "Thanks. I needed that."

"Anytime you need to be insulted, just come to me,"

she said, sitting back, letting herself be aware of him as a man again, not a client.

She saw him check her out, something he always did, always seeming…interested. No, it went beyond that. *Attracted.* She'd been wondering for a long time how it would feel to make love with him—since before she knew what making love really meant.

"What's next, Laura?"

"Give me the rest of the day to study her estate issues. Do you have a will?"

"Yes. It's in Joe's safe."

"Bring it to my office tomorrow, and any other documents you have. Life-insurance policy, brokerage account information, whatever else you can think of. Do you own a home?"

"I don't own anything. I have investments, of course."

"You'll want a trust drawn up. And you need to decide on a guardian, should something happen to you."

He didn't say anything for a few seconds, then pushed himself out of the chair. "I should get back to Ethan and Millie."

Laura handed him the portfolio, minus the documents she needed, and followed him to the door. "Give my office a call in the morning. I'll fit you in." She gave his shoulder a friendly pat, then let her hand linger long enough to feel his muscles tense. "What are you going to do?" she asked.

"Get to know my son."

"And after that?"

He turned around, breaking contact. "I don't know. This particular scenario hasn't been on my what-if list. Thanks again for letting me interrupt on your day off."

"No problem. Donovan? How do you feel, finding out you're a father?"

"Bonded. Possessive. Worried. I don't want to mess up, you know? He's already been through more than any little boy should."

"Don't expect perfection of yourself."

"Why should I expect less than usual?" He half smiled. "I know I have a lot to learn, Laura, and I'm probably going to mess up along the way. I'll count on you to point out when I'm falling down on the job."

The last thing she wanted was to get close enough to him to do that. She would do her job as his attorney, but that was it. "I'm sure your big, boisterous family will let you know," she said.

"Family sees a different truth from friends."

She considered that, understanding what he meant but deciding not to keep the conversation going, because she had an urge to hug him, to get body to body with him—and not just to comfort.

Laura watched him drive off then returned to her house. She still had plenty of time to relax by the pool before she started on Donovan's case, but she was more anxious to dig into Anne Bogard's life—and to get the job done. She couldn't afford to spend a lot of time with him.

She'd already surprised herself when she'd stopped by this morning to tell him goodbye. Her relationships were casual for a reason. A very good reason. She wasn't marriage material. Period. She said as much to every man she dated, believing in full disclosure. Some men were grateful and continued a casual relationship, others backed away.

The end result was always the same, anyway—they left. Which hadn't caused her any heartache. *Yet,* she thought, as she picked up Donovan's paperwork and headed for her office.

By the time Donovan returned to Joe's house, not only was Joe there, but their older brother, Jake, too. They both were sitting in Joe's truck in the driveway.

As Donovan approached the truck, the brothers climbed out—Joe, ponytailed and athletic, and Jake, newly married and a father to two-month-old Isabella. He looked like the adventurer he was, long and lean, with dark brown hair and probing blue eyes.

"Joe filled me in," Jake said.

"I don't suppose you helped me out by telling Mom and Nana Mae, too?" Donovan gave Joe a steady look.

He laughed. "I left the easy stuff to you, Donny."

"Right." He glanced toward the house. He wasn't as reluctant to tell his mother as his grandmother. There had never been a McCoy born out of wedlock. She would have something to say about that.

"How do you feel?" Jake asked.

"Probably about the same as you when you came home and found Keri nine months pregnant."

"Turned out okay for me."

"I expect it's going to turn out okay for me, as well." He was grateful to have Laura helping, too. "Do you want to meet him?"

"I thought you'd never ask."

The three brothers were headed to the house when a car honked. Donovan recognized that horn. His mother and grandmother were back from Sacramento.

Aggie McCoy, a sixty-seven-year-old widow of ten years and the dictionary definition of "mom," leaned out the driver's window. "Why're you still here, Donny?"

His brothers gave him I'm-sure-glad-it's-you-and-not-me looks. He walked over to the car and crouched, greeting his mother and his paternal grandmother. "I have some news."

Before he could tell them, the front door of the house opened and Ethan stepped onto the front porch, stopping there.

"Ethan." Millie came up beside him. "I told you to stay inside."

"I waited and waited. He didn't come in."

The image of Ethan standing hopefully at the window jarred Donovan. He had a lot to learn about fatherhood. "It's all right, Millie. I'm sorry I kept him—and you—waiting. Please join me."

Millie took his hand, nudging him forward.

Donovan set a hand lightly on Ethan's shoulder. This

time he didn't flinch. "Mom. Nana Mae. This is Ethan. My son."

"Well, of course he is," Aggie said, opening her car door and getting out as Jake went around the car to help their grandmother out.

"And this is his grandmother, Millie Bogard."

Aggie ignored Millie's outstretched hand and hugged her instead, one of her classic all-engulfing hugs. Donovan knew his mother must have a ton of questions.

Nana Mae came around the car on Jake's arm, using her bright purple cane to help steady herself on the other side. "I'm Maebelle McCoy," she said, her voice strong. Then to Ethan, "I'm your great-grandmother. Everyone calls me Nana Mae."

Ethan stared wide-eyed, keeping his hand firmly in Millie's as the introductions continued with his uncles.

"Ethan, would you go inside with your uncles and Grammy for a minute, please," Donovan said. "I need to speak to Grandma Aggie and Nana Mae. I promise I'll be there in a minute."

"Okay," he said, looking relieved, then racing ahead of the adults.

When the door shut, Donovan took a steadying moment. "I'm sorry I didn't get to warn you. I didn't have any warning myself. They just appeared. I'm hoping you won't mind if they stay with you for a few days, Mom. Me, too, for that matter, while we all make the adjustment."

"Of course I don't mind. Where's his mother, Donny?"

"She died a month ago. Anne Bogard."

"Without telling you about Ethan?"

He nodded. "I'll explain later. For now I don't want to keep him waiting. He's still unsure."

"Well, of course. There's plenty of time."

He turned to his grandmother then. "I'm sorry, Nana Mae. I know he's the first McCoy born out of wedlock. I hope you won't hold it against me, since I didn't know myself."

"You should have."

Her tone wasn't accusatory or angry, but matter-of-fact. And it silenced him. He should have taken the time to find out before he wiped Anne out of his life, as she had him. It was irresponsible of him.

"You're right," he said to his grandmother. "No excuses."

She patted his cheek. "You'll be a good father. I always knew it."

She headed toward the house, taking careful steps, refusing his arm, giving him a moment with his mother.

"How can I help you the most?" Aggie asked.

"I don't know yet. Opening your house to us is the first step. I have a lot of decisions ahead."

"Including about your job."

"Especially that. I can only imagine what Nana Mae would think of me if I left anytime soon."

Her blue eyes, the exact same color as Donovan's,

twinkled. "I've been Maebelle McCoy's daughter-in-law for forty-nine years. One thing I know about her—she'll love you no matter what."

The front door opened. Ethan stood there, waiting, silently reminding Donovan of his promise to meet him in the house in a minute.

"And so it begins," his mother said.

She was right. It was a new chapter, probably the longest one in his book of life, but at this point, mostly blank pages waiting to be written on.

Chapter Four

Millie and Ethan went to bed at eight o'clock, exhausted from their long journey and the emotional roller coaster of the day. Restless, Donovan took off for a walk. He considered his options. He could go to Joe's house three blocks away and have a couple of beers while they watched a Giants game, giving his overloaded mind a break from the relentless thoughts bombarding him. But he was tired of noise. He needed some quiet, which was rare for him.

It wouldn't be dark for another half hour or so. He walked the streets of his hometown, seeing it anew. He'd always appreciated the beauty of the place. Nestled in the foothills of the Sierras, the land was green, the air clear. The miners who'd come to the Mother Lode of this part of California in the 1850s had not just mined for gold, but settled the town. Many of the houses built over the years since still survived. Those who built new generally chose designs to fit in with the surroundings, whether Victorian or contemporary log cabin.

Donovan passed a house with a for-sale sign in the front yard, a smaller "offer pending" tacked across it. Jake and his new wife, Keri, had made an offer, having decided to move into town from Jake's cabin outside the city limits. The old Braeburn house had been vacant for months, ever since the Widow Braeburn had been moved into a nursing facility, so the transition into the four-bedroom Victorian should be quick.

Donovan turned right at the corner and realized he was a block from Laura's street. He wished he had a reason to stop by, but he hadn't even gathered all of the paperwork she wanted, was still waiting for some information to be faxed or e-mailed before he went to her office tomorrow.

He could've kept going past her block and on to the park nearby, but instead he intentionally walked toward her house. She was out front, watering the garden herself, using a hose instead of her in-ground sprinkling system. Donovan couldn't name many flowers beyond roses and daisies, much to his landscaper-brother Joe's disgust, but it didn't take knowledge of the names to appreciate Laura's yard. It bloomed with mostly pink and purple flowers, punctuated here and there with a few white blossoms. Her cottage-style house was small, white and homey. He would've expected something more sleek and contemporary for her, not this cozy place. Even the neighborhood was mature, with few families, mostly just singles or older couples.

You're making yourself old before your time, Laura Bannister.

Her back to him, she couldn't see him coming up the sidewalk. She also wore earbuds connected to a music device in her pocket. She'd changed back into the cool shorts and tank top she'd been wearing early that morning when she'd stopped by in her car.

Donovan couldn't take his eyes off her. There was a reason she was called The Body. A man could put his hands anywhere on her and enjoy either full curves or smooth planes. Her skin looked touchably soft, as did her hair.

He came up behind her, tapped her on the shoulder to get her attention.

She spun around, using her hose as a weapon, and soaked his shirt.

He shouted a laugh, grabbed the nozzle but ended up turning it on her. She shrieked, yelled his name and danced away, as he angled the nozzle toward the ground. She reached over to turn off the faucet, then plunked her fists on her hips and scowled.

She looked magnificent.

It was the first time he could remember seeing her ruffled. Well, the first time in fifteen years, anyway.

"Sorry," he said.

"I'll bet."

He smiled. She could win any wet T-shirt contest, anywhere, hands down, especially with that nice lace bra revealed.

A couple of teenage boys rode by on bicycles, staring. Donovan eased in front of her, blocking their view. One wolf-whistled. The other crashed into a parked car. Donovan looked at Laura, whose eyes sparkled. He laughed.

She crossed her arms, but he could see she'd relaxed.

"I *am* sorry," he said. "I hadn't intended to get you wet. I was just reacting."

"I believe you. It's funny you came along when you did. I'd just been thinking about you, wondering how you were doing, hoping you were okay. You already needed time away?"

"He's asleep. He and Millie were wiped out. And, yes, I needed some time alone." He moved past Laura and wound the hose on its reel. "I suppose you're used to that kind of reaction. Those boys," he said.

"It's no different from yours." She walked up the steps to her front porch. "You're just quieter about it. You always have been."

He followed, even though she hadn't actually invited him. "You check me out, too."

She made a noncommittal sound, then opened her

door and went inside, leaving it open, which he took as an invitation. He followed, shutting the door behind him.

"I'll toss your shirt in the dryer, if you want," she said before disappearing down the hallway.

His shirt wasn't soaking wet, just a wide stripe down the middle that would probably be almost dry by the time he walked home. But since it suited him to hang around awhile, he peeled his shirt over his head and waited for her to come back.

When she returned, she'd changed tops. As she walked by him, she swiped his T-shirt out of his hands. He followed as she went into the kitchen and then the laundry room at the other side. She gave his bare chest as much of a look as he'd given her wet T-shirt out front.

It made him smile. He liked a woman who was sure of herself, sure of her sexuality, someone who could match him in bed, sometimes taking over. She would be a match.

He also knew they were treading in dangerous waters. The interest had been there for years. It wouldn't take much for it to get much more personal.

Or maybe she was just getting even for what had happened—had *not* happened—years ago, and had decided to tease him with the intent to reject him. Well, it didn't really matter. He needed a distraction, needed not to think about Ethan for a little while. Or Anne. Laura was as fine a distraction as he could ever wish for.

The dryer started tumbling and she returned to the kitchen, where he stood looking out her window. It was almost dark.

"How about a glass of wine?" she asked.

He would've preferred beer. "Sounds good."

She poured from a bottle already opened. "Shall we sit outside by the pool?"

"And let the mosquitoes use us for appetizers?"

"They should be gone by now." She passed him a wineglass, then led the way to the backyard. They settled in two lounges, didn't say anything for a few minutes. He wondered what her thoughts were, since his own were deeply involved in a graphic fantasy.

"How was the rest of your day?" she asked finally.

He tried to focus again. "Um, it was good. He's a great little kid, and not surprisingly overwhelmed by all the new people in his life. We kept it to a minimum, but we'll add more tomorrow. He's got cousins a few years older, so that's going to be helpful. And he's gone to preschool since he was three, so I figure he's pretty well socialized."

"He's accepted you already?"

"No. I didn't mean to imply that. But one good thing Anne did was to tell him about me. She'd even shown him pictures. And Millie did some research, found out I was here and had talked to him about me during their trip, and about the fact she would be going back to England. She laid good groundwork."

"I'm surprised she didn't contact you first, rather

than just showing up. Or let you come to them, instead, and be in his own environment."

"So was I, but I figure Anne must have assured her I wouldn't shirk my responsibility. Or Millie decided a surprise attack would be best." Anger swooped in and pecked at him, as it had many times during the day. He'd missed five years with Ethan. Five long years.

"It looks like you'll be sticking around Chance City," Laura said. "Any decisions on your job?"

"I won't go anywhere for a while, that much I know. We need time together, for the two of us and for him to get to know his family. I want him to feel comfortable and settled first."

"There's nothing you could do here or from here?"

"There are probably jobs to be found, but something I'm interested in? Passionate about? I sure haven't come up with any ideas."

"I've heard that most journalists are frustrated novelists. Any interest in writing a book?"

"I've thought about it." He had contacts. Maybe now was the time to put out feelers. "I've got enough based-on-a-true-story material to write ten thrillers, but I'm not sure how well I'd do being cooped up in front of a computer all day. I love being in the field, interviewing people, getting into the action."

"Getting injured. Fearing for your life. Mmm-hmm. I can see the appeal."

He laughed. "It's rarely that touch-and-go."

"So you exaggerate in your articles?"

"You read my work?"

Her mouth tightened, as if she'd revealed something she hadn't wanted to. "I subscribe to *NewsView,* and you write frequently for them."

"They pay the best."

"What will happen with the Mexico job you were headed to today?"

"It gets put on hold. No one else will write the story, if that's what you mean. It's not as time-sensitive as some. I've been in touch with my editor at *NewsView.* He understands what's going on." He gestured toward the surroundings. "You've created quite an Eden for yourself."

"My decompression tank." She sipped her wine. "Have you read Anne's journal yet?"

"Started to. It's pretty painful at the beginning, so I put it aside for now."

"I can't imagine being in your shoes, finding out you have a child after all this time. It must be very helpful having your family."

He stared into space, considering her words. "I think it's harder in some ways." He turned toward her, set his wineglass on a nearby end table. "It's like there's a spotlight on me, following my every move. Everyone will want to have input, you know? All five of my sisters have children and are not shy about offering advice—ever. All but one are older than me, have always mother-henned Jake and Joe and me. My oldest sister, Cher, is fifteen years older than I am, got married at eighteen, has children in their twenties. It's a helluva formidable group, this family of mine."

"I would have no idea what that's like."

He knew her father had left when she was young, so it had been only her and her mother. Laura had always been a loner, even in high school. Donovan graduated three years ahead of her, so he'd only gotten news about her secondhand, from Joe. She'd never tried out to be a cheerleader or run for class office. The boys teased her, as teenage boys always did, not knowing how to deal with a smart, beautiful girl like her. And the other girls didn't welcome her into their groups, probably because they felt threatened by her.

When it came down to it, though, it'd been her responsibility to find friends for herself, and she hadn't done it. On the other hand, she'd ended up as valedictorian, gone on to college and entered beauty pageants, winning the Miss California title, then Miss U.S.A., then was first runner-up for Miss Universe, shocking everyone. Not just because she'd done so well, but because she'd put herself out there like that when she'd stayed behind the scenes in high school.

Then she'd gone to law school and had been practicing law ever since, here and in Sacramento. But even now, she stayed on the fringes, showing up at events, yet not doing anything to call attention to herself.

"I didn't mean to bring the conversation to a halt," she said, setting her empty glass next to his. "When I said I wouldn't know what having a big family was like, I wasn't whining. I was stating a fact."

"I didn't take it that way. I got lost in thought, that's all. And I'm not saying I'd trade my family for anything, just that in some ways I'd like to take off with Ethan and not come back until we've gotten to know each other first, without others interfering."

"Why can't you do that? He won't start kinder-garten for a over month. Take some time."

"I'll think about it. Thanks for inviting me in, Laura. I didn't know how much I needed to blow off a little steam." He grinned. "Although I do know of better ways to do it."

She gave him that sexy lawyer look. "I'm your attorney."

"Okay, so, once everything is handled and you're not my lawyer anymore?" He tried to look as if he were teasing her, making a game of it, when he was abso-lutely serious.

"Unless you take your business to someone else, I'll still be your attorney. It's unethical."

"Meaning, if I fire you, you'd be interested?"

The dryer buzzed, loud and long. The ensuing silence slowly refilled with the sounds of crickets and frogs, seeming to chastise Donovan personally for his foolishness.

He sat up and swung his legs over the side of the lounge. "Are you seeing anyone right now?" he asked.

"My answer doesn't matter. Ethics do."

"Humor me. It's not like you're representing me in a murder trial, you know."

"No," she answered lightly, then stood and headed into the house.

No, she wasn't seeing anyone? Or *no,* she wasn't going to humor him by answering?

After a minute he smiled, gathered the empty wine-glasses and followed. He rinsed the glasses and set them on her kitchen counter just as she came into the room with his shirt and handed it to him.

"Thank you," he said, moving closer to her. "We've got unfinished business."

"Water over a very old dam, Donovan."

He watched a vein throbbing visibly in her neck, a noticeable reaction to their conversation.

She took a step back. "What part of 'I'm your law-yer' don't you understand?" she asked, even as goose bumps rose on her skin.

He backed away, drawing his shirt over his head and down, then apologizing.

"Accepted," she said.

"You'll still be my lawyer?"

"Of course."

"Damn."

She laughed, which was what he'd intended.

"Bring Ethan and Millie with you tomorrow, please," she said.

"Sure. Good night, Laura."

"Night."

She shut the door right away behind him, so there was no awkward moment of whether to turn back and wave. She'd already dealt with it.

He made the walk to his mother's house, his thoughts in more turmoil than when he'd left. He never pushed women, had always accepted no as a final answer. Yet he'd pushed Laura to the point that she'd had to remind him about ethics. Him, of all people.

His mother was seated in a rocking chair when he climbed her porch steps. "Everything okay?" he asked.

"Quiet as clouds. Poor little tyke. What a big day he had."

Donovan eased onto the porch swing, crossed his feet and set it in motion, his arms stretched along the back. The stars had come out. Not the brilliant blanket it sometimes was when there was no moon, but a scattering.

"Big day for you, too, son," Aggie said.

"Yeah. Big day." Whatever event might have taken first place in his life before had been drop-kicked into second now.

"You'll need to register him for kindergarten right away, so there's a space for him. Carly said she'd go with you, if you want."

"I'll manage on my own, thanks." And so it began. Sisters already taking charge.

"Ethan'll need a physical. Doc Saxon can do it."

I know, I know. "Millie brought his medical records,

including immunizations. Should make the transition easy. I need to get him on my health insurance."

His cell phone rang, his brother Jake.

"Good news," Jake said. "We got the house. We'll officially have a fifteen-day escrow, but they said we can move in tomorrow, if we want, and just assume that all the paperwork will go through fine."

"That's terrific."

"It is, but what I'm really calling about is to ask if you want to live at the cabin. We decided to keep it as rental property."

Jake's one-bedroom-with-an-office log cabin would be perfect. It was off the beaten path a little, so he and Ethan would be separate from the rest of the family but still close enough to keep the connection tight.

"That'd be great, thanks, Jake. Perfect. How soon can that happen?"

"The more help you give, the sooner you can move in."

He laughed. "I knew there'd be a catch."

"You would've helped, anyway."

Yeah, he would have. "Do I have to paint?"

"Probably. And Keri's been making noise about some new fixtures in the bathrooms. That job you had with Bud Hollenbeck could come in handy."

Bud was the best, although slowest working, plumber in town. Donovan has spent one summer working with the man. It had settled Donovan's mind about getting out of town, since the jobs available to people here in the tiny bedroom community were mostly in the trades or tourist related. He'd had different dreams.

Jake had left home because he felt he didn't fit. Donovan had a calling.

"You never forget how to seat a toilet, do you?" Jake asked, laughter in his voice.

"Unfortunately not."

"We'll give you the first month rent free for your help."

Money wasn't an issue, which Jake knew. Donovan didn't own anything, had invested and saved, because his job wasn't exactly the most secure. "It's a deal. I walked by there a while ago. House looks in pretty good shape, but the yard needs work."

"Keri's dying to get her hands into the earth. *Her* earth, she's calling it. She wants to be planted, then let her roots go deep."

After a few more minutes Donovan hung up. Aggie smiled. "They got the house?"

"Yep. And he's offered to rent me the cabin."

He saw the disappointment in her eyes. She liked having them all staying with her. With so many children and grandchildren, people were in and out of the house constantly, but it wasn't the same as having someone living there, someone she could pamper—and mother.

The screen door creaked. Ethan pushed it open an inch and peeked out.

Donovan hurried over. "You okay, buddy?"

"I just wanted to make sure you were here."

Progress. "I'm here. Do you want to sit with me for a while?"

"On the swing?"

"Yes."

"Okay. But not in your lap."

Donovan was hungry to hold him, to comfort him and keep him safe, but he did what Ethan asked, just picked him up and set him on the swing. He brought his knees up and wrapped his arms around them.

"Hi, Grandma," Ethan said quietly.

"Hello, little man."

Ethan giggled at that, then nestled his chin on his knees.

"Did something wake you up?" Donovan asked.

"Mum did."

Donovan glanced at his mother, who lifted her brows. "Did you have a dream about her?" he asked.

"No. She was here. She sat on my bed and talked to me."

"What did she say?"

"That she loves me." He said the words matter-of-factly.

"That's nice." What could he say to that? "Um, do you see her a lot?"

"Just sometimes. She doesn't look sick anymore, so why can't she come back?"

Donovan closed his eyes for a moment. His first big test. "It's good that she doesn't look sick anymore, isn't it?"

He nodded his head against his knees.

"But you know that when someone dies they don't get to come back, right?"

"I know."

"We usually only have pictures and videos of them. You're pretty lucky that you see her now and then. But she can't come back, not like before, anyway." He put a hand on Ethan's back, glad that he accepted the touch easily. "But she'll stay with you the rest of your life, Ethan, in your dreams and in your heart. She'll never stop loving you. Okay?"

"Okay." He yawned, then after a minute, leaned against Donovan. Pretty soon he was asleep.

Donovan scooped him up and carried him to bed, tucking him in, kissing his head. He stood over his son for a few minutes, watching him sleep, his heart pounding, love flowing.

"Well done," Aggie said when he returned to the porch.

"Thanks."

"You know it's just the beginning of the questions, right?"

"I guessed as much. I figure I need to be as honest as possible, as I would with anyone else."

"Just trust your instincts. You'll do fine."

"I feel like I have to have better instincts than the average person, Mom. I'm coming into this late. I wasn't given a chance to start at the beginning and grow with it."

"You'll see. It'll be okay."

It had to be, he thought. Because failure wasn't an option.

Chapter Five

From her desk, Laura watched Donovan pass by her office window. She couldn't see the boy or his grandmother, but assumed they were beside him. He was taller, and probably blocked the view.

Laura heard the front door open. She smoothed her hair as Donovan greeted her mother, Dolly, who ran the Chance City office. Usually Laura would walk into the reception area to greet her clients, but his voice was enough to freeze her in place.

She'd done little else but think about him last night and this morning, especially the way he'd looked stretched out on her lounge, shirtless.

It was like being in high school again, a time when

she'd trailed him in the hallways, trying not to let him see her, her heart thumping. Then when she'd finally worked up the nerve to talk to him—

A boy bounded into view and stopped, framed by her doorway. Donovan was right. There was no doubt about paternity.

Ethan smiled. Laura smiled back and went to say hello to him. She rarely interacted with children, the exception being children of clients, and Donovan's baby niece, but then Laura didn't have to figure out what to say to an infant.

"My name is Laura," she said. "What's yours?"

He stuck out his hand. "Ethan."

"Very nice to meet you," she said, shaking his hand.

"Very nice to meet you, too."

He had a sweet smile and wonderful manners, which spoke highly of his mother.

"Good morning, Laura."

She looked up, tried to put on an expression as busi-nesslike as her blue suit. "Hello, Donovan. Ethan and I have introduced ourselves." She extended a hand to the woman at his side. She was probably in her early fifties, slender and blond, with rosy cheeks and soft blue eyes. "I'm Laura Bannister."

"Millicent Bogard. Call me Millie."

"Please come in."

Ethan climbed onto the chair in the middle, then spotted a display case in the corner and hopped off to go look at the contents. "Wow! You must be the Queen of America."

The case contained some of her sashes, crowns and even a scepter. She knew it was too much like bragging, but her clients got a kick out of having a beauty pageant winner as their attorney. And this was her hometown, after all. Her most prestigious prizes were in her home office.

To Laura they represented so much more than winning a pageant. They'd meant financial survival through college and law school.

She joined Ethan at the case. "They're all kind of flashy, aren't they?"

"Sparkly! That one's brilliant," he said, pointing to a scepter and sounding very British. "I could fight with that. Take that! And that!" He mimed dueling with a phantom partner, his expression intense.

"Ethan," Donovan said, caution in his voice.

He stopped, then trudged back to his chair. "I *know*. Behave." His tone was long-suffering.

Laura made eye contact with Donovan and smiled, as did he. She took her seat behind her desk and thumbed through the papers he'd stacked there.

"I hope I brought everything," he said.

"I'll check it all out later." She turned to Millie. "I'm so sorry for your loss."

"Thank you. Anne was lovely. A little headstrong, you know, but a lovely girl, and a good daughter."

Ethan climbed from his chair and onto Millie's lap,

his sneakered feet bouncing so much that Millie had to lay a hand across his shins. Laura saw yearning in Donovan's eyes.

"Ethan," Laura said, then waited for him to focus on her. "What do you think of your new town?"

"It's good."

"You have a great big family now." Laura tried to imagine it. Her mom meant the world to her, but the idea of so many siblings and cousins was daunting. Especially since the McCoys were always in each other's business, and she liked her privacy.

Ethan looked serious. "Grammy says they're like friends but better. I only met my uncles and Grandma Aggie and Nana Mae. But we're having a party tonight and everyone will be there. You can come."

"Please," Donovan prompted, looking just as hopeful as Ethan.

"Pleeease." Ethan dragged out the word, grinning ear to ear.

Laura felt backed into a corner. The McCoys were famous for their big family parties. Even spur-of-the-moment, as this one would be, there would be tons of food, plenty of noise, and spontaneous dancing. "Maybe I can drop in for a little while," she said, hedging.

"Will you bring that?" He pointed to her scepter.

"Ethan, that's like a trophy for Laura," Donovan said. "You know what a trophy is?"

He nodded hugely. "I got trophies for soccer and T-ball."

"You wouldn't want anyone to play with them, would you? What if they got broken?"

"I wouldn't like that."

"Okay, then."

Laura was satisfied that Ethan was making the transition into his new life just fine. Not that she could've done anything about it, but she'd had enough experience dealing with broken families that she could recommend counselors. At the moment, she didn't think it necessary.

"Did you meet my mother out in the reception area?" she asked him.

"That's your mum? She's pretty, too."

"Thank you," Dolly said from the doorway, fluffing her red hair dramatically. "How about you come play with me for a while, handsome?"

He looked at Millie, who said, "We won't be long, love. And I saw a basket of toys out there."

He left the room with Dolly, who shut the door behind her.

Laura turned to Millie. "Is there anyone who might try to claim that Ethan should be with them instead?"

"Donovan's his father. No one disputes that."

"That fact doesn't necessarily stop people from trying to make a claim. Not that Ethan could be taken away, but legal battles can happen. It's…inconvenient. And expensive. Did Anne have a significant other who might challenge Donovan?"

"No. No one. Oh, she dated some, but Ethan was her whole life, even before she got sick."

"And are you asking for anything from Donovan?"

Millie's eyes widened. "Like what? Money? Anne left me some. I don't need more."

"I noticed that in the trust. I was thinking more along the lines of visitation requests."

"Let me step in here," Donovan said. "Millie can come visit as often and for as long as she wants. If she wants to move here, I'll help her get settled. And if coming here isn't feasible for her, I'll make sure that Ethan goes to England to visit."

"That's very generous, Donovan," Millie said, her eyes taking on a sheen.

"You're his grandmother. You're his direct connection with Anne. That's important."

"Thank you."

"Do you have any questions?" Laura asked Millie.

"Anne's lawyer answered all that I had before. Is there anything I'll need to sign? Because I expect to be leaving day after tomorrow."

"Already?" Donovan asked, his surprise evident.

Millie patted his arm. "You've seen how he turns to me instead of you. It'll help if I'm out of the picture." She looked expectantly at Laura then.

"If I come across something in the paperwork, I'll let you know in time, Millie. Now, if you don't mind waiting in the reception area with Ethan, I need to speak to Donovan for a minute."

"Of course."

"Alone at last," Donovan said, a few seconds later, setting the tone. He smiled, slow and sexy.

She resisted his flirting. "I thought we settled this last night. Are you going to continue to tease me, knowing nothing can happen between us?"

"My time will come. I'm just keeping you primed for that moment."

She laughed. She wished she didn't feel flattered by his attention, and wasn't totally drawn to him in every other way, especially watching him in the role of father. Her father had left when she was two, with promises to visit often, according to her mother, anyway. He'd never come back.

"So, Millie's leaving," she said, changing the subject.

"That was the first I'd heard of it. I'm sure she's right about it forcing Ethan and me to become a unit, but I think she's also anxious to go home. She's been caregiver for a long time. I imagine she needs some time for herself."

"While you no longer have time for yourself." She couldn't imagine what that would be like, having someone totally dependent on her. She didn't even own a pet.

"True."

An interesting response. A statement of fact only. He was good at that.

She opened a folder. "Who are you naming as Ethan's guardian?"

"Jake and Keri."

"They've agreed? I know that seems like a dumb question. It's a technicality."

"They've agreed."

"Actually, you need to designate two guardians— one for Ethan, and one for the estate. It can be the same person, or you can choose someone else for the estate. Sometimes it's better that way. No emotional involvement."

"You mean, like you?"

"Yes. Or anyone else."

"Let me think about it. I'll let you know."

"When you've decided, I'll give Jake a call. We'll need to adjust for this change in his own estate documents, in case something happens to him."

"We sure plan for a lot of contingencies."

"Planning pays off."

Donovan nodded. "Have you heard that Jake and Keri are buying a house around the block from you?"

"Which one? There are a couple in different directions." She almost held her breath, waiting for his answer.

"The Braeburn house on Poplar Street."

Relief eased into her refilling her lungs. Not the Denton house.

"Ethan and I will be renting Jake's cabin for now."

Which meant he wouldn't be in town anymore, but a ten-minute drive away. No more going out for a walk and stopping by. Which was probably a good thing, given their attraction.

"Good for them. I know Keri wants to be closer to

the action—and the family," Laura said. "I reviewed everything you gave me yesterday. Anne's trust is straightforward. I'll get the transfer of funds started."

"I want all of Anne's money to go into a trust for Ethan."

"Including the insurance payout?"

"Yes."

"Okay. Payable to him at what age?"

"Twenty-five. I can lower that later, if I want, right?"

"Of course. Or raise it, for that matter. But don't you want it available to him for college?"

"I'll take care of part of that, and he can earn part of it."

Laura knew he'd made his own way in the world, without help from anyone, so it didn't come as a surprise that he would want Ethan to do the same. "All right. I think that's it for now. I'll call you if I have questions."

"And you'll come to the party tonight? It's at Mom's."

"I'll try."

"Laura, you told Ethan you'd come. You can't disappoint him."

"I told him *maybe*." A tiny bit of panic struck her. She didn't want to get too involved.

"You'd better believe he didn't hear the maybe." Donovan stood.

Laura came around her desk to walk him to the door. "I feel a need to caution you. I've observed a lot of situations where children come into a new household, whether it's foster kids or newly adopted—which is similar to what you're experiencing. There's generally a honeymoon period where kids are extremely well behaved or extremely badly behaved. Ethan is going to feel abandoned. You can't avoid that. So, just know that how he acts now, especially after Millie leaves, isn't necessarily how it will be when he settles in. Be patient and, above all, be consistent. You'll find your own path together."

"Thanks. I've already noticed he's much more comfortable with women, which says a lot about how he's been living." They had reached the door. "This is the Laura I know," he said, touching her hair briefly. "Hair up, business suit, makeup, heels. I've seen another you, a more relaxed you. Which one rules?"

"Different looks for different occasions, but still all me."

"Layers."

"I certainly hope so." She spoke quietly so her words wouldn't breach the door.

"Say you'll be there tonight, Laura."

"I'll be there." She didn't have to stay long, after all.

"And you'll stay more than ten minutes." He grinned. "Yes, I've figured you out a little."

She didn't want to fall for him, but he was making it difficult. She liked his boldness. He was a brilliant reporter, honored and respected. He hadn't gotten that way by sitting back and waiting for something to happen.

"I'll stay at least fifteen," she said. "What can I bring?"

"I heard you don't cook."

"No, but I shop very well."

He smiled. "Why don't you just bring yourself? We'll have tons of food. Six o'clock."

She wouldn't go empty-handed. "That's a sweet boy you've got."

He nodded, then opened the door. Ethan looked up, his expression hopeful. "There's an ice cream shop next door. Did you know?"

"I had no idea."

"My favorite is chocolate. Grammy likes vanilla."

"Good to know."

"I have money, you know," Ethan said. "Grammy gave me some."

Donovan knelt down to him. "I was having fun with you, son. I'd be happy to treat you to an ice cream. Want to come along?" he asked Dolly.

"I never pass up an ice-cream cone."

"Laura?"

"I have a client due any minute."

"We're only going next door."

She was being a stick-in-the-mud because she didn't want to get close to him, and to Ethan. There were good reasons not to. Excellent reasons. Sanity-saving reasons.

"Next time, maybe," he said, ending the silence. Then they were gone, and the office seemed enormous and quiet.

She returned to her inner office and desk. After a few

minutes she heard the front door open. She went to greet the expected client, but it was Donovan, carrying an ice-cream cone, mocha almond fudge, her favorite.

He didn't say a word, just handed her the cone and left. As he opened the door, her client approached.

"Hey, George. Laura's running about ten minutes late," Donovan said, throwing his arm around the man's shoulders. "Come have an ice cream with me first."

"If you're sure."

"Positive. Laura won't mind."

The door shut behind them. Donovan winked at her as they walked by her window.

And Laura sat in her chair and savored the ice cream for the full ten minutes, trying to remember the last time she'd just had fun with a man. It'd been a long, long time.

Chapter Six

The McCoys were spread out for Ethan's welcome party from Aggie's front yard, to inside the house and on into the back. Donovan watched over Ethan as he played out front with a few of his cousins, a little shy but warming. He was the youngest by several years. Most of the women were in the kitchen putting the final touches on their potluck items, laughing and teasing each other, their voices drifting through the screen door.

The sound was familiar and relaxing.

Even though they'd just given him a send-off barbecue two days ago, everyone seemed happy enough to be back for more. And if Ethan was a little overwhelmed by the number of relatives, he didn't show it beyond a little extra clinging to Donovan's hand. Ethan probably would've been clinging to Millie, instead, but she'd busied herself with the food preparation, purposely making herself unavailable to him.

Only two non-McCoys were there—Millie and Dixie Callahan, Joe's ex-fiancée, who'd recently moved in with Nana Mae to help care for her, without Nana Mae knowing she was being taken care of.

Donovan was on the lookout for the other non-McCoy invited guest, Laura, and to watch Ethan ride a bicycle with training wheels that one of the cousins was passing down.

Everyone came with gifts, all of them in grocery bags, for which Donovan was grateful. He didn't want to sit and unwrap gifts for an hour. But he admitted to being curious about what kinds of things they'd brought.

He spotted Laura from a block away. It was an especially warm evening. Maybe her skin would be pink and dewy from the long walk....

She was wearing another formfitting summer dress, the neckline not too low, the hem midthigh. She'd left her hair up. He'd bet if he commented on it, she would say she was cooler with it off her skin. He didn't really mind, because it exposed her long, tempting neck, but he did like the messy look he'd seen yesterday after she'd been sunbathing at home.

He moved to the sidewalk to greet her, noting that she also came with a Nordstrom shopping bag, but he could see colorful wrapping paper inside, with kid-appealing robots printed all over it. Ethan pedaled up, coming to a stop between them.

"Hi, Laura!"

"Hello, Ethan. Looks like you're having fun." She smiled at Donovan but quickly returned her attention to the boy.

"Guess what? I'm related to all these people. I have aunts and uncles and cousins." He leaned close to her and whispered, "I can't remember everyone's name yet."

"Maybe they should wear name tags until you do."

He scrunched up his face. "That's silly."

"Why?"

"Because I can't read."

After a moment, Laura started to laugh. Ethan chimed in, giggling in delight, not really getting what made it funny, but going along with it.

She reached into her bag and pulled out a package. "This is for you."

"It's not my birthday for a whole month."

"We talked about this, son," Donovan said. "It's a welcome party. I'm getting presents, too. But you have to wait until later to open the packages."

The boy sighed. "Thank you, Laura, but I have to wait until later."

"No problem." She slipped it back into the bag.

"We're about to eat," Donovan explained. "Presents after dinner. Mom's rules. It drags out the anticipation." Which worked in his favor, because it would force her to stay through dinner and beyond. It would seem rude if she left before Ethan opened his gift from her. Sometimes life just worked out perfectly.

"Dinner's on!" someone yelled through the screen door.

"Hey, bud, ride your bike through the gate into the backyard," Donovan said, "so it's not sitting on the sidewalk."

"Okay." He took off, leaving Donovan and Laura to follow.

"Thanks for coming," he said.

"My pleasure. He looks happy."

"It's an ongoing process."

"And you? Are you happy?"

He hesitated long enough that she stopped, putting her hand on his arm to halt him, too.

"What?" she asked. "You aren't happy?"

"It's not that. I can't say this to anyone else." He shoved his hands in his pockets. "I'm in over my head, you know? I have all these nieces and nephews, but I've never spent much time with them, and certainly never been responsible for them. Joe's got all the kid experience, since he's never left Chance City. I know he babysat when he was a teenager. Even now he takes the kids places. Fishing, ball games, lots of different activities. I don't know how to relate."

"From what I've seen, you're relating just fine. In fact, I'd say you're a natural."

"I haven't been tested yet. It's all fun and games so far." He put his hand at the small of her back, urging her forward so they could join the family in the backyard, then didn't let his hand drop until they were almost in sight of everyone. Her dress was damp where he touched her. Something about that aroused him. Maybe just the vision of them working up a sweat while they made love—hot summer nights made even steamier in bed sharing body heat.

He wondered if part of her allure was that he couldn't have her—

No. He'd avoided her during the two months he'd been home because he knew it couldn't go anywhere, and he wanted his visits home to be uncomplicated. It'd been a conscious choice. He'd rather ignore her so that he wouldn't sleep with her than have to ignore her because he *had* slept with her.

Donovan watched his mother sweep Laura into a hug, saw Laura stiffen and pull back as soon as she could. She fished a bottle of wine from the paper sack she carried and gave it to Aggie, which made Donovan smile. His mother would put it aside for a special occasion, and probably never serve it because it was way too special.

Donovan let Laura fill her plate, waiting for her to come back to where he'd saved a seat for her. She surprised him by not even looking his way, but heading to where Dixie and his new sister-in-law, Keri, sat, the two women a study in opposites. The curly-haired blonde, Dixie, was about five-five and blessed with the perfect hourglass figure. Dark-haired Keri stood a couple of inches taller and was reed slender, having lost the pregnancy weight in a hurry.

Putting Laura between them defined the contrasts even more. She was taller than Keri, blonder than Dixie and a perfect balance between Keri's slenderness and Dixie's voluptuousness.

Donovan filled his plate, then sat at a picnic table, glancing at the women occasionally as he ate, wondering how they'd all become friends, then deciding that while they were different from each other in visible ways, there were similarities. All three women were comfortable in their own skin, and were confident and strong—matter-of-fact, no-punches-pulled women. He'd always recognized what Joe had seen in Dixie all these years, and couldn't believe he'd let her get away. As for Keri, Donovan had come to recognize what Jake saw in her, how she made his life better, richer. It had taken Donovan a long time to trust her, but it was part of his nature to be skeptical.

Yet he already trusted Laura.

"You look like you've got dessert all scoped out."

Donovan jolted at the sound of Joe's voice as he sat beside him, his own plate heaped with fried chicken and potato salad. Donovan gave his brother a quelling look. "You know I never turn down cherry pie."

Joe laughed. "Is that what you call Laura? Cherry

pie?" He picked up a drumstick and eyed it casually, too casually.

"You can't say I don't have good taste," Donovan replied, knowing it was useless to argue the point.

"Nope. Sure can't. I can still picture her in that bikini she wore to David Falcon's party."

"Me, too," Jake said, joining his brothers. "I almost asked her out a few times over the years, but I had a feeling she'd chew me up and spit me out. You're a braver man than I, Donny."

"Don't you have a baby to take care of?"

"Isabella is sleeping. Where's *your* child?"

Donovan stood in a hurry. He'd been so wrapped up in sneaking glances at Laura, he'd forgotten Ethan.

"He's fine," Jake said, exchanging a grin with Joe. "He's sitting on the grass over there with part of our village." He pointed to where Ethan sat with five of his cousins, smiling tentatively.

Donovan lowered himself to the bench again, feeling like an idiot, but knowing his brothers wouldn't embarrass him in front of the others. Parenting was a brand-new role.

"What time are we getting started tomorrow on your house?" Donovan asked Jake.

"Smooth change of subject." Jake grinned. "Early. So far, I've lined up about fifteen people. We'll paint tomorrow, and pull up carpet. There are hardwood floors under the carpets. We're hoping they won't need too much work. We figure we can be set up and moved in within ten days. But we've got a ton of stuff to buy. We plan to leave most of the furniture that's at the cabin. Is that okay with you?"

"Are you kidding? That'd be great."

"You'll need a bed for Ethan." Jake turned his head at the sound of a baby crying. He stood, then went to meet their sister Darcy, who held and bounced Isabella as she came out of the house. Darcy turned sideways, not letting Jake take her. She kept moving toward Keri. Jake followed.

Donovan watched in amazement as Laura reached for the baby instead of Keri. Almost instantly, Isabella quieted.

"The baby whisperer," Joe said.

"What?"

"That's what they all call Laura."

It was news to Donovan. He hadn't figured her for a kid person at all, but especially babies. She generally left kids alone, although she certainly seemed at ease with Ethan. "I didn't know she was that close to Keri. I've seen them talking at some of the parties, but that's all. She was at Jake and Keri's wedding."

Joe picked up his empty plate and Donovan's to toss. "Laura turned thirty this year, like Dix and me. Maybe she's looking for a change. Trying to get involved more."

Donovan zeroed in on Joe. "Does that mean you're looking for a change?"

Joe shrugged. "I've been doing the same thing for a whole lotta years, you know?"

"To great success."

"Yeah. That's the problem." He started to walk away, then turned back, a hint of a smile on his lips. "Can I get you some cherry pie?" He gave Laura a quick glance.

Donovan wished it was that easy—just order her up and she would appear. She would be sweet and tart, too, just like his mom's pie.

Joe didn't wait for an answer. He didn't have to.

Ethan came running up. "Is it time to open Laura's present now?"

"Five more minutes, bud. Let everyone finish eating."

"But—"

"Patience, Ethan. There are a lot of gifts to open, not just Laura's."

Ethan walked back to where his cousins sat, kicking the ground as he went. Donovan smiled at the universal body language of being denied something. He shifted his gaze to Laura, who still held the baby but was watching Ethan. She made eye contact with Donovan and smiled, too; then Keri said something and Laura passed her the baby.

Donovan waited to see if Laura would join him, since he was alone now and she no longer held the baby, but she continued to sit where she was, looking back at him, the smile on her face leaving by degrees.

He wanted her. He wanted to see her naked, to kiss her for hours, to seek the warmth inside her and find satisfaction. Then he wanted to do it again.

A plate of cherry pie dropped with a thud on the table, then Joe landed beside him. "You've got it bad," he said. "You know she's untouchable."

"That should stop me?"

Joe raised his brows. He scooped up a forkful of lemon meringue pie, his favorite. "I forget how much of a pit bull you can be."

"Did Dixie make the lemon pie?" Donovan asked innocently.

Joe ducked his head. "Tastes like hers."

"Are you ever going to fix things with her?"

His younger brother continued to eat without comment.

"Okay, if you're not going to fix it, are you going to start dating?"

"Maybe."

"You're in a tough spot."

"Yeah," Joe said. "The hazards of living in a small town."

"Dixie's in the same position, I imagine. Are you sure there's no hope? You've got sixteen years invested in this relationship."

"Like I don't know that?"

Donovan saw Ethan make his way to Laura and lean against her armrest. They talked easily. Ethan kept trying to see around her to the baby, but Isabella was nursing, and covered by a blanket. Keri looked peaceful in the midst of all the noise and chaos of the McCoy clan.

A loud whistle pierced the air—Nana Mae. It always made Donovan laugh to hear her, now eighty-nine, whistling like a stevedore, a skill she'd passed down to most of her grandchildren and great-grandchildren.

"Thank you, Nana Mae," Aggie said from where she stood under the patio roof. "I think it's time to open presents, so if Donny and Ethan would join us, please?"

With a small, embarrassed-looking smile, Ethan came across the lawn to hop into one of the chairs on the patio, next to a table stacked with bags.

Donovan joined him, but the whole time they unwrapped gifts, he kept an eye on Laura. He couldn't let her slip out. Not when he intended to walk her home.

Ethics be damned.

Chapter Seven

Father and son approached the whole present-unwrapping event with similar reluctance, Laura noticed. Ethan peeked into bags first then drew out the contents, whether it was a new toy, a used toy, pajamas or a bathing suit, with the same shy look.

"It really isn't my birthday yet," he said once, drawing laughter.

Donovan seemed almost embarrassed for a while, too, then got into the spirit of the moment. He'd been gifted with a box of "It's a Boy" cigars, a first-aid kit, coupons from several people for babysitting, a booster seat for the car and lots of products to start his own household—kid shampoo and pump soap, but also the other basics like dish soap and laundry detergent, and other kinds of cleaning products and utensils.

Laura had given them a pass to a family fun center in Sacramento, where they could play miniature golf, ride bumper boats and drive race cars.

Her gift to Ethan was the last one unwrapped. He ripped open the colorful paper to find two plastic swords upon which she'd glued a whole lot of fake gems. She'd had so much fun tracking down the toy swords in just a few hours and then decorating them like her scepter.

"Wow! Donovan, look! Brilliant, isn't it? Thanks, Laura."

Everyone went silent. Ethan noticed. He looked around. Donovan slipped an arm around his shoulders. "Maybe you could call me Dad."

Ethan looked unsure. "Oh. Okay. Dad."

Donovan ruffled Ethan's hair as people began talking and moving around, clearing off serving dishes. Laura decided to slip out, but she couldn't leave without telling Aggie goodbye and thank you.

"You're not leaving yet, are you?" Donovan asked, coming up beside her.

"Isn't it over?"

"Nope. We're just going to make room to dance."

"I don't dance." She just wanted to get away from the noise, to have her quiet house envelop her. Calm her. Having spent the evening watching Donovan—

"You don't dance?" He said it as if she were un-American or something.

"I have two left feet."

He looked down, then shook his head. Music filtered from outdoor speakers. People partnered up—husbands and wives, adults with kids, kids with kids. The song was neither fast nor slow, but that awkward tempo in between. He took her into his arms.

"Donovan, please. I really don't want to do this." But he'd already pulled her close, drawing her body-to-body with him, and suddenly she wanted to be there, even if she stepped on his toes.

"Not so bad, hmm?" he asked.

She didn't answer. Couldn't answer. Her heart was lodged in her throat. Every nerve ending did pirouettes throughout her body. But she was also aware that a lot of people were watching them. So while she wanted to lean against him and use the excuse of dancing to snuggle close, she pulled back a little, putting some space between them, and stumbling over his feet at the same time.

He laughed, low and sexy. "You're so obvious."

She met his teasing gaze. "About what?"

"About wanting me. You'll even trip just to get closer."

"In your dreams."

"Oh, yeah. Dreams, for sure." He whispered into her ear, "Hot ones. Detailed ones."

Laura had dated a lot, but no one like Donovan. However, she had always been direct at the beginning of the relationship, never really allowing any man to court her, or tease her, or tantalize, as Donovan was doing, but keeping things simple instead. She didn't know how to respond to his…wooing.

"Are you going to fire me?" she asked.

"I can't. Yet."

Ah. There it was. The anticipation. He was an expert at creating it. He was putting her on notice that once his legal needs were met, the professional relationship would be terminated and a more personal one would begin. She was safe as long as she continued to do work for him.

"I wonder how often you're speechless," he commented idly.

"I wonder how often you're humble."

He laughed then, full-throated and appreciative— and everyone looked, and smiled.

"I need to go home," she said, moving out of his arms, keeping a composed smile on her face for appearance's sake. He didn't try to talk her out of it, so she was able to say goodbye to people, including interrupting Ethan's swordplay with a cousin to give him a hug.

Laura walked through the side gate and out to the street. It wasn't dark yet, but the air had cooled to a more comfortable temperature than on her walk over. She hadn't gone twenty feet before Donovan jogged up beside her. She stared straight ahead, not acknowledging him. He kept silent, too, just matched her step for step.

She tried not to laugh. Tried hard. She'd almost succeeded when he started whistling "Ain't She Sweet."

She laughed then, and shoved him. His eyes twinkled.

"Why aren't you home, putting your son to bed?" she asked, choosing a safe topic.

"The party isn't over. He's still playing. Your gift was perfect, Laura. It opened him up. Did you notice that?"

She'd noticed he'd gotten more comfortable as the evening went along, but didn't consider her gift the catalyst. "I probably should've asked you first if you objected to toy swords."

"I don't know what I do or don't object to yet. I'm taking it day by day. But as a former boy myself, I think it's fine." He was quiet for a while, then, "He called me Dad."

She heard the emotion in his voice. "I gathered that was the first time. It was kind of cute how he called you Donovan."

"It sounded really strange, coming from him. I have to keep reminding myself that he just lost his mother, and I need to be careful not to push him about anything. It was spontaneous. We hadn't talked about what he should call me."

She squeezed his arm. They walked along in silence for a block or so.

"You don't like crowds much, do you?" he asked.

"No."

"Are you claustrophobic?"

She could say yes, use it as an excuse, but it wasn't the truth. "No."

"I've seen you at a lot of events, large and small. You're never in the middle of the action."

"Is that worthy of a headline?"

"I'm curious. You're personable, you don't seem shy, yet you hang back."

A lot of people jumped to incorrect conclusions about her, mostly based on her pageant wins, as if that would turn her into an extrovert. She'd entered pageants to earn prize money and scholarships, and had come out at the end of law school debt-free. Not many people could say that.

"I apologize, Laura," he said. "That probably sounded like criticism. I really am just curious. I mean, you go to these events, but don't participate, so, naturally, I wonder why."

"Sometimes someone railroads me into going," she said, eyeing him. "Even uses a child to do it."

"I'm always looking toward the goal. That's my fatal flaw."

"You mean winning."

"Is there a difference?"

They kept walking, past homes where children played in front yards and parents sat on porch swings, watching. Most people waved. Small Town, U.S.A. It did still exist. Not that everything was perfect. There was crime, of course, but people really did look out for each other.

"Want to stop by Jake and Keri's new house? Peek in the windows?" Donovan asked.

"Sure."

Suddenly the quiet between them seemed peaceful. Natural. She relaxed.

"This is nice," he said after a while.

"Yes."

Silence again. And it was okay again. When they reached the house, they walked up the steps to the porch. The curtains were pulled aside.

"Looks like we'll be having a garage sale," Donovan said, peering in. "Jake said the house comes as is. That's a lot of furniture in there."

"*Old* furniture."

"Antique?" he asked.

"Maybe, but doubtful. If it'd been valuable, someone in the family would've taken it out. You've all got a lot of work ahead of you."

"You wanna come help?" He bumped shoulders with her. "I could line you up with a pressure washer. You could wear your world-famous bikini and spray down the siding."

She shook her head. "You never give up."

"There'll be time for that when I die."

She admired his attitude, frankly, but she wasn't about to give him ammunition when he created enough on his own. "I'll be helping Keri, I'm sure, but it'll be after work hours. I'm in Sacramento two or three days a week, remember." Maybe she would invite everyone for a swim when they were done. She could pick up food from a deli near work and bring it home with her.

"I've noticed that you and Keri, and Dixie, too, for that matter, have been hanging out," he said.

"Yes." She'd been making an effort to have girlfriends, something she'd been missing, always afraid to reveal herself to anyone. Almost every relationship she had was superficial, and she'd come to recognize that—and be appalled by it, even though she knew the reasons why.

"That's it?" Donovan asked. "'Yes'?"

"Yes, I have been hanging out with them more," she said, teasing him.

"You are tough. I'd like to see you in action in a courtroom."

"I don't end up there often. Only if a divorce case gets really nasty and we have to take it to court to resolve it. I pride myself on being able to get people to come to a determination without it going that far, though. Most of the time I can follow through."

He sat on the top step, inviting her with a gesture to join him.

"Is that part of your reputation, then? Negotiating amicable divorces?" he asked, waving at a couple out walking.

"Those are also extremely rare. A couple may start out thinking they can keep things cool between them, but it doesn't always work. Where emotions are involved, there's always reaction. Plus, friends and family interfere, as well, a big cause of difficult divorces. But I do my best to keep things on task, especially where kids are involved. So many of them get so hurt."

"Did you become a divorce lawyer because of your own parents' divorce?"

She tucked her hands in her lap. "I do family law, which isn't exclusively divorces, but pretty much you're right. It was ugly."

"So that's what drives you?"

"Partly. Been there, done that. It helps."

"You never saw your father again?"

She pulled her body closer, clasping her hands tighter, leaning forward more. "No. Never."

"Do you know if he's alive? If you have half siblings somewhere?"

"I have no idea."

"Never wanted to find out?"

She eyed him directly. "Hey, newsman, just because you have a huge, loving family doesn't mean those of us who don't are searching for that. I've never felt denied."

He hesitated a few beats. "You're right. I apologize. And, believe me, sometimes I think you're the lucky one."

She would like to see him at work. He adjusted quickly to changes in conversation and situations, probably a critical skill for a top-notch journalist who needed to experience something in order to write about it to his personal standards, especially in war-torn countries.

Laura admired that about him. A lot. The list of pros about him kept growing.

She stood. "You should probably head back so you can tuck your son into bed. I'm fine walking home from here."

"It's on my way back to Mom's." He stood, as well, then placed his hand on the small of her back as they headed up the walkway.

As it had earlier, the touch of his fingers sent her pulse racing. Need filled her, almost painfully.

Maybe she would be the one to fire *him* as a client....

She stopped that thought cold. "How do you think Ethan is going to react to Millie leaving? Has he talked about it with you?"

"He alternates between being okay with it, probably because he's been so busy, and being sad. He understands that she's going. I don't think he really understands how far away she'll be, and that she can't just drop in. Fortunately, we'll have Jake's new house to work on, and then getting settled in the cabin, and then kindergarten. It should keep him busy."

"So, you're not going to take him away for a while?"

"I decided not to. We'll have privacy at the cabin. And he'll need people around him, too. He tends to seek out women. That's his comfort level. I don't want to interfere with that transition. I don't know, Laura, I'm just trying my best to figure out what works. I'm used to knowing what I'm doing. I'm not sleeping well, I can tell you that."

They reached her house and stopped at the head of the brick walkway. "Thanks for the company," she said. If she'd had pockets, she would've stuffed her hands in them. She clenched them into fists instead. "I'll give you a call when your paperwork is ready."

He did jam his hands in his pockets. His gaze dropped to her mouth. He took a step closer, still staring, slowly moving up to her eyes.

She waited, logic having taken a vacation from her brain, desire filling the space instead. She'd always loved his mouth....

"Good night," he said. He eased around her and headed down the street.

Laura let out a long, slow breath. She'd wanted him to kiss her. Wanted it bad. She would've let him, too, right there on the street in front of her house. In public.

Shocked at herself, she moved toward her house. Her phone was ringing when she opened her front door. When she picked it up, all she heard was someone whistling "Ain't She Sweet." She listened until he let the last note fade out into one long, drawn-out sound. She hung up the phone gently.

It should've made her smile. Instead, her throat burned and a lump formed. She went into her office and pulled her high school yearbooks off the shelf, sat cross-legged on the floor and thumbed through them, something she hadn't done in years—probably since she'd graduated.

Her hair was perfect in every photograph she came across of herself, her smile exactly the same. Her pageant smile, she realized. Teeth showing, eyes vacant. She found Donovan's senior portrait. He looked confident. Cocky. She found other pictures of him—student-body president, newspaper editor, debate team, homecoming king. Big man on campus.

She closed her eyes, remembering the day she'd finally worked up the nerve to approach him. Lots of boys had pursued her, but she knew it wasn't for her mind. Donovan hadn't given her a second glance, which was probably why she wanted him. She figured he would appreciate that she had a brain and could use it, not be intimidated by her. And she thought he was the hottest guy on campus, wanted him without knowing exactly what it was she was wanting. She knew the basics of the birds and bees, but she'd had no idea she could lose all common sense over a guy.

He certainly had no idea how much it had cost her to go up to him in the school parking lot and introduce herself. Determined not to wait a day longer, she'd been waiting for an hour before he finally showed. His was the last car there.

"I know who you are," he'd said.

"I really like you," she'd blurted.

"Uh. Okay." He jingled his keys in his pocket and looked around. *Now* she could recognize that he'd been looking for someone to rescue him from an awkward situation. But that was then.

Maybe a smart girl would've noticed and not forced the issue. She was smart, but not about boys. "I'd like to kiss you."

His eyes widened. He took a step back. But she lunged, planting her mouth on his. He grabbed her arms and moved her away from him. "What the hell are you doing?" he asked. "Are you crazy?"

She was. Crazy in love with a boy she knew nothing about, just that she wanted to be with him. "You don't have a girlfriend. I asked."

"So?"

"So, how about me?"

He frowned. "What are you offering, exactly?"

"What would you like?"

Laura could almost laugh about it now. She'd been so naïve. Her knowledge of sex was minimal, just a concept she'd seen in books and movies. She didn't understand the emotional commitment it entailed, good or bad.

"Look," he'd said calmly, being much more mature than she. "I'm flattered, okay? But you're too young, you know?"

He'd softened the blow by telling her that. She recognized now he'd just been being kind to her, letting her down easy.

"And in two months," he'd added, "I'll be out of here. I'm not coming back."

"Why?"

"Because there's nothing here for me except my family. I want to travel the world. I want to do something important. Don't you?"

She hadn't known yet. She was only a freshman in high school. How could she know what she wanted three years down the road? Still, she would have two months to change his mind. If she worked at it, she could do that.

"I want to be with you," she said.

"I don't know how else to tell you I'm not interested," he said, clenching his jaw, his frustration with her finally letting loose. Then he'd gotten into his car and driven away, leaving her standing in the empty parking lot, her face red, her heart broken. She'd never approached a boy again. Never went on a date in high school. Lots of boys looked, but none of them asked her out. She had an invisible *Go Away* sign on her forehead.

Then a month after she graduated, she learned she had uterine cancer, a secret only she and her mother knew. Her world had turned upside down, and hadn't fully righted itself since.

And now family man Donovan McCoy was the last man she should get involved with.

The problem was—she wanted him as much now as she had at fifteen. She should be discouraging him, but she couldn't seem to do that as she could with any other man.

She closed the yearbooks and set them aside. She couldn't have him then because he had bigger plans for himself. She shouldn't have him now because he would want more than she could offer.

That left her stuck in limbo, attracted but unable to act on it. And dangerously close to falling in love with a man she shouldn't love, one who shouldn't love her back.

Because she could never give him what he wanted most, even if he didn't realize it yet—a family.

Chapter Eight

The night was mid-July hot. No breeze stirred the air. The sun would set in an hour, bringing a welcome drop in temperature. Until then, Laura's swimming pool was the best place to be.

Donovan sat on the edge with Joe, their feet in the water, which couldn't really be called cool. Wearing a life vest, Ethan clung to Donovan's ankles and bobbed in the water. A few teenage nieces and nephews played Marco Polo at the other end.

Most of the family had spent the past two days sanding, painting, cleaning and decluttering. They would hold a garage sale the next day, Saturday. Aggie would run the show. She loved wheeling and dealing.

Joe elbowed him. "Are you as disappointed as I am?"

"About what?"

"That Laura's wearing a one-piece bathing suit."

Donovan studied her as she refilled a potato-chip bowl and talked to Keri, who had Isabella in her arms. No, he wasn't disappointed—well, he was disappointed for himself, but he was content that no one else was seeing her that way. She wore not only a one-piece but a loose, hot-pink blouse over the plain black suit.

"I hadn't thought about it," he finally said to Joe, who laughed. He'd obviously been goading Donovan.

"Much," Donovan amended. It'd been a nice surprise when she'd stopped by Jake and Keri's house to invite them all for dinner and a swim when they were done. About half of the family accepted the offer. The pool was full.

Nana Mae came through the back door then, Dixie with her. Dixie hadn't been able to help much with the house because she attended cosmetology school in Sacramento during the day, but she would undoubtedly help over the weekend. Despite the awkwardness between her and Joe since she'd broken off their engagement, she was still one of the family. Longevity counted.

Guilt dropped over Donovan's shoulders as he watched Nana Mae settle in a chair. He hadn't spent any time alone with her since Ethan had arrived. Donovan needed to change that before she started giving him The Look, the one she'd directed at any of them when they'd misbehaved as kids. The Look was much more effective than anything she might shout.

Too late, he realized. She was giving him The Look right then. Even from across the pool he could see her crystal-blue eyes firing displeasure at him. Donovan had been on the receiving end of that particular expression much more than the rest of his siblings.

"Come in the water with me and play," Ethan said. He'd stayed close to Donovan ever since they'd taken Millie to the airport that morning, but hadn't called him Dad again yet.

"Please," Donovan reminded his son.

"Pretty please, with a cherry on top."

Donovan slipped into the pool. Ethan climbed on his back and clung to his neck, his chin resting on Donovan's shoulder.

"I miss Grammy," he said.

"Of course you do."

"When can I see her again?"

"Probably at Christmas. But you can call her, you know."

"Now?"

"She isn't home yet. It takes a long time to get to England from here. She'll call us when she's home."

Ethan moved his hands from Donovan's neck to his shoulders, relaxing a little. "Let's go pull Laura into the water and play with her."

The idea appealed to Donovan, too, although differently. "An excellent plan, my boy." He swam quietly toward where she'd taken a seat on the edge, watching Jake dipping Isabella in the water, her arms and legs moving wildly, splashing water everywhere.

"*Laur*-a!" Ethan shouted in a singsong voice. "We're coming to *get* you."

Donovan grabbed her ankle before she could get away. She yelped. Ethan giggled, a joyful sound to Donovan's ears. Then she fell into the water with a splat, sputtering as she surfaced.

"We *got* you," Ethan said happily.

"His idea," Donovan added.

"And a four-year-old boy holds all the power? You couldn't say no?" She shoved her hair out of her eyes, and kept that now-familiar forced smile on her face.

"I'm almost five."

"Yeah. He's almost five." Donovan loved when she got on her high horse about something.

She tried to pull off her wet blouse. Donovan helped her, then tossed it onto the deck. By the time she turned around, any signs of annoyance were gone. She stole Ethan away from him, and they went off and played. Appreciating how she'd turned the tables on him—and knowing when to admit defeat—he got out of the pool and went to visit his grandmother. Dixie had just hopped into the pool, too.

Donovan wiped the water from his face, kissed Nana Mae's cheek, then sat in the empty chair next to her. She wore a new hairstyle, a frequent occurrence now that Dixie was there to fix her hair every morning.

No more mass of permed curls, but stylish, chic looks that took ten years off her.

"You've been avoiding me," she stated.

"Guilty."

"Am I so formidable?"

He sort of laughed. "You even have to ask?"

"I don't mean to be." She looked puzzled by the very idea of it.

"You don't know the reach of your power, Nana Mae."

"Power? Me?" She thought it over for a minute. "Okay. I'll accept that, since I think you're really talking about respect. Anyway, that's no excuse for ignoring me."

"I have no legitimate excuse, except I've been busy." He leaned back, keeping an eye on Laura and Ethan as they held hands and jumped up and down. Maybe she'd had the notion that by wearing a one-piece black suit, she wouldn't draw anyone's attention, but seeing her jump like that? If he was alone, he would salute.

"Yes, dear, I know you've been busy, which is why I'm not going to pester you about it. But as soon as Jake and Keri have moved into the house, and you've moved into the cabin, I expect to see you."

"I'll take you to the Lode for lunch."

"That would be lovely."

"I'm sorry I disappointed you," he said then, getting the worst of it out of the way now, not wanting to have it festering between them.

She settled her purple cane in front of her, resting

both hands on the crook, looking thoughtful. "I know the McCoy legacy carries with it a lot of pressure, Donny—no children out of wedlock and no divorces. But I think the very fact that legacy exists has made us all more careful, more responsible. Even the ones who marry into this crazy clan feel a different expectation for themselves. It doesn't hurt."

"And I didn't live up to that expectation. No one regrets that more than I do, since I missed five years of my son's life. I didn't get to see his birth, or celebrate all those firsts."

"Do you think marriage to Anne would have worked?"

"I would've made it work."

"She seems very selfish."

"Self-protective, I think. And angry. But also selfish," he decided. "So was I."

"You still would've done your duty."

Yes, he would have. But would he have been happy? Content? Enjoyed forever-after love? They were questions without answers. He was into fact, not speculation. "I'd prefer not to discuss Anne anymore. What's done is done, and she's not here to defend herself."

His grandmother stared into his eyes for a few long seconds, then patted his cheek. "You're a good boy."

"Thank you."

"And you've got eyes for Laura Bannister, I see."

"I'm male."

She laughed, then looked toward Laura. "That girl could use a good, strong partner at her side."

"That *girl* is stronger than most men."

"Maybe. But don't equate strength with need. She needs the same things that everyone else does."

He didn't want to get into it with his grandmother. He didn't even know how he felt about Laura, except he wanted to strip her naked and not let her out of touching range for, oh, say a year or so. "How about letting me figure out one life crisis at a time?"

Her eyes twinkled. "I believe I can do that."

"Your hair looks very nice," he said, turning to another subject. "Must be nice having a live-in hairdresser."

"I'd rather she and Joe got back together. I've tried to talk to her about it, but she threatens to leave whenever I bring it up. And it's not that I need someone living with me, you know, but I do enjoy her company. Plus, the reason she came to stay with me in the first place was to be able to go to school full-time. She's so close to finishing."

"Here's your prune," Laura called out, sending Ethan toward Donovan, who grabbed a towel and wrapped him up. As warm as the evening and the pool were, Ethan was shivering, his body having had enough of the water.

Taking a chance, Donovan lifted Ethan into his lap and held him close. For once, he didn't even squirm, making Donovan very happy. How could he love someone so fast, so completely? It hadn't taken more than a minute and would last a lifetime.

As they waited for Ethan to stop shivering, Nana Mae tried to talk to him, but she was the only person who turned him shy. He would nod or shake his head to answer a question. He spoke if he had to, but with as few words as possible.

Laura climbed out of the pool then, emerging like some kind of water goddess. She tilted her head to one side and wrung out her hair. Her bathing suit gaped just enough to tease.

"You should get Laura a towel, Dad, and let her sit on your lap for a minute. I'm all warmed up."

Nana Mae laughed quietly. Donovan didn't dare look at her.

"She'll be fine, bud. She wasn't in the water as long as you."

"Oh. Can I get a cookie?"

"Just one. We need to leave pretty soon."

"Aw, man."

Donovan didn't know how he felt that Ethan had learned that particular phrase from his teenage cousins. He didn't want Ethan growing up too fast.

Ethan slid off Donovan's lap and scurried over to the food table, choosing a cookie about the size of his face, it seemed, and probably the equivalent of four cookies.

The pool emptied out, the long, hard workday catching up with everyone. No one asked if they could help clean up, they just did, even as Laura kept trying to tell everyone to leave it. Hadn't she been around his family enough to know that wasn't how they did things?

He saw her finally give up and accept their help. She'd tied a brightly colored skirt around her waist that undulated as she moved. He caught her looking at him several times as he and Joe moved patio furniture back in place, while at the same time keeping an eye on Ethan, who had curled up on a chaise.

Laura grabbed a dry towel from a stack she'd put out and tucked it around him, bending to whisper something in his ear. He smiled, but his eyes remained closed.

"Looks like they've bonded," Joe said.

"I think she's a safe haven in a sea of rowdy McCoys. He's still working at sorting us all out."

"Either that or he's as infatuated as you are."

Infatuated? Was that it? Donovan was on fire for her, certainly. And he got a kick out of riling her to see her reaction. She smelled good, too, which always drew him closer. He liked when she stood her ground as much as he liked that she sometimes got nervous enough to back away. Infatuated? It was a good enough description, he supposed.

Joe dropped a hand on his shoulder, bringing Donovan out of his stupor. "I'll give you a ride home. Looks like Ethan will be deadweight to carry."

"Thanks. I need to tell Laura goodbye first."

He tracked her down in the kitchen, alone, everyone else gone except for Joe. She was bent over the dishwasher, adding silverware, her very nice rear in his direct line of vision. She sure made it hard to resist her. He must have made a noise, because she spun around.

"I figured you'd already gone," she said.

"Without saying goodbye? My mother raised me better than that."

"According to your mother, you were the most stubborn, independent, doesn't-play-well-with-others child she bore."

"That's probably true. But I still learned manners." He moved closer. "To say please. To hold doors open. To tell the hostess goodbye."

She didn't say anything, just watched him suspiciously.

"And to say thank you." He bent close and kissed her cheek.

She went absolutely still. He felt a moment, just the tiniest moment, where she leaned into him, her hand brushing his arm as if to steady herself.

He moved back. Their eyes met. Hard to resist, for sure.

"You're welcome," she said in slightly more than a whisper. "I had fun, too."

"See you tomorrow?"

She found her voice. "I imagine so. I told Keri I'd put new shelf paper in the kitchen cabinets."

"I'm in charge of installing the new toilets."

"Sounds fun." Her eyes twinkled.

"I'm flushed with anticipation."

She laughed then, and he decided to leave on that note.

He was aware of her following him into the backyard

and saying goodbye to Joe. Donovan lifted the sleeping Ethan into his arms, then headed for the front door. Joe preceded them, so the door was already open. Donovan stopped to give Laura one last look. She ran a hand over Ethan's hair. Donovan felt her other hand slide down his spine, stopping at the small of his back, as he had done to her a few times.

Get the damn paperwork finished up, he ordered her silently. He wanted to see where this relationship could go.

She smiled as if aware of his thoughts and her own power, maybe even happy to be causing him discomfort? "Good night, Donovan."

Like hell it was going to be.

Chapter Nine

A week passed, during which Donovan ran into Laura now and then, usually at Jake and Keri's house. Every time, he would ask how the paperwork was coming along. Every time, she would say, "Patience."

The anticipation was killing him, was even interfering with the decisions he needed to make about his future. Consequently, for the first time in his memory, he was procrastinating. He and his brothers generally took after their father, a man who'd worked hard, never missing a day on the job until he keeled over and died of a heart attack at the age of sixty-one. Donovan was twenty-three when it happened, and every year the loss grew bigger.

"Daydreaming?" Jake asked, coming up behind Donovan as he finished installing a new medicine chest in the master bathroom, the last job on his to-do list. Tomorrow the new furniture would be delivered, and they could begin to settle in and make it theirs.

"Thinking about Dad."

Jake leaned a shoulder against the bathroom door-jamb. "He's been on my mind a lot, too."

"How does it happen that I miss him more now than ever?"

"You've been too busy until now? You're a father yourself?" Jake looked around. "He would've loved working on the house with us."

A carpenter turned general contractor, John McCoy had lived for moments like this—family helping family. Pitching in. Getting the job done quickly, but doing it right.

"Do you think he was happy?" Donovan asked.

"Who?" Joe asked, coming up beside Jake and peering into the now-completed bathroom.

"Dad," Jake and Donovan said at the same time.

"Of course he was happy." Joe stepped around Jake and into the room. "What a change. Does Keri like it?"

"Keri is thrilled," the woman in question said, joining them, sliding her arm around Jake's waist. He pulled her close. "It's sparkling clean, too. Did you do that?" she asked Donovan.

"Your husband did the honors."

She angled closer to Jake, setting her hands on his chest. "I find that incredibly sexy."

Jake laughed, then kissed her.

Donovan hadn't had that kind of relationship in a long time, if ever. That playfully sexy banter and teasing-foreplay kind of rapport. His longest relationship had been with Anne, and it'd been intense and serious.

"Hey!" Donovan said. "I put up the cabinet. Don't I get a kiss for that?"

"Get your own girl," Jake said, tucking his wife against him.

"I can think of one," Joe said.

Keri smiled. "Me, too."

Donovan felt like a teenager, but he asked anyway. "Does she talk about me?"

"Not one word."

He tried to swallow his disappointment.

"She's very good at keeping confidences, you know. Comes in handy in her profession."

"I agree, but how does not saying anything mean she's interested?"

"It's something she *could* talk about. She chooses not to, which gives it more importance, at least in my book."

"Plus there's that whole X-rated-look-in-her-eyes thing," Joe added.

"That, too," Keri agreed lightly.

Donovan's cell phone rang, displaying Laura's office

number. "Are you ready to toss ethics to the wind?" he said instead of hello.

A beat passed. "Well, not today, but I'm free tomorrow."

Crap. Not Laura, but her mother. "Hi, Dolly."

"Hey, sugar." She was laughing like crazy. So were his brothers and sister-in-law.

"What's up?" he asked.

"Laura wanted me to notify you that your papers are done and ready to be signed. If you want to stop by and pick them up, you can have the weekend to read through them. Then we'll arrange for some witnesses when you sign on Monday or Tuesday, or whenever you want."

"Okay, thanks. Sweet 'ums," he added.

She laughed as she hung up.

He looked at his watch. "I finished my official to-do list," he said to Jake. "Anything else you can think of?"

"I'm sensing there's somewhere else you'd like to be."

Donovan shrugged. "Only if you really don't need me for a few hours."

"Take the whole day, if you want. You've already done more than I would've thought humanly possible."

Donovan *had* pushed himself all week—as a distraction, as a way to vent frustration, and, of course, to help Jake and Keri get moved in as soon as possible. As much as he loved his mother, he was ready for his own space, and to build his relationship with his son.

On his way home, he stopped by Laura's office, making a detour next door first.

"Hey, there, sugar," Dolly said, grinning.

"Hey yourself, sweet 'ums. I brought you a bribe." He handed her a strawberry ice-cream cone.

She reached for it. "I'm taking a lick first, just in case I can't go along with whatever favor you're going to ask and I have to give it back."

He smiled. He didn't know Dolly well, but he had, on occasion, wondered how such a gregarious woman could be Laura's mother. Or maybe the point was that he didn't know *Laura* well enough.

Donovan started to speak, but Dolly held up a finger. "One more."

He sat in the chair across from her desk. "Go ahead and finish. I'll wait." He whistled tunelessly, looking around the room.

With one bite left, she hesitated, the bottom inch of the cone in hand. "What do you need?"

"Laura's in her Sacramento office today, right?"

"Right."

"I need for you to get me an appointment with her late this afternoon."

"That's all?" She popped the final bite into her mouth. "You didn't need a bribe for that."

He leaned back and crossed an ankle over his knee. "Well, there's a little more to it."

Her brows arched high.

"I don't want her to know I'm coming."

"Afraid she won't see you otherwise?"

"*Sure* of it."

She drummed her fingers on her desktop, studying him, then stopped abruptly. "Okay. Under what name?"

"Cory Spondent."

It took her a second, but then she laughed, a big shout of appreciation. "You don't think she'll figure out it's you?"

He grinned back. "Not until it's too late, I hope."

"She's pretty smart."

"It's something I admire about her."

"I figured you would. Okay. So, what reason can I give her assistant for your appointment?"

"Trust."

"That you want to have her put a trust together for you?"

"No. Just trust."

Her smile turned soft. "Okay." She picked up the phone and made the arrangements, then passed him a large packet that had been sitting on her desk. "Four o'clock. Her assistant's name is Moses. He likes butterscotch sundaes. No walnuts. He's allergic."

"Good to know." He stood. "Thanks, Dolly."

"Donovan? She's put up some pretty solid walls."

"I've noticed. Patience isn't usually a virtue of mine."

A thoughtful look came over her face, as if debating what to say. He waited. Sometimes he could be as patient as Job.

"I'm going to paint you a picture," Dolly said finally. "Do you know that house on Denton, the big old white Victorian?"

"Sure. Wraparound porch. West windows face the park. In complete disrepair."

"Exactly. When Laura was a little girl, we used to walk by there on our way to the park, and she would always stop and stare at it. She called it the *It's a Wonderful Life* house. Not because it looked exactly like the movie one, but because she thought having a house like that would give her a wonderful life."

He got it. She might appear to be sensible and logical, but inside there was a dreamer, too. He needed to remember that.

"So," Dolly said. "Even though patience isn't one of your virtues, try."

Or leave her alone. He heard the unspoken request as clearly as if she'd said it.

What she didn't know was he'd never wanted like this. And he wasn't about to deny himself unless Laura said no.

He didn't think she would say no.

"Your last appointment is here." Moses stood just inside Laura's door.

She glanced at her computer, pulled up her daily calendar. "Did you already give me a file on…" She read the name, Cory Spondent. "Cory. It's a *him,* I assume?"

Moses, twenty-six, tall and as skinny as a birch tree,

looked flustered, a first for the usually cool, easygoing man. "I forgot."

Speechless, she stared at him. He never forgot anything. Ever. "Are you okay?"

He nodded.

"Can you put a file together while I'm talking to him, please? It's a trust he's interested in, right? He's—" She stopped, her gaze zipping back to the computer screen. Cory Spondent? She laughed.

"Send Mr. McCoy in, please. And I'm sure he'll want coffee."

Moses stood aside, and Donovan came in, a manila envelope in hand, obviously having been waiting just outside the door instead of in the reception area.

"Cory Spondent?" she said, gesturing to him to take a chair opposite her desk. She knew why he'd come. So did her body. Blood raced through her, scorching hot. Almost two weeks—plus fifteen years—of anticipation swirled and stormed.

"You laughed," he said. "I heard you."

"Well, of course. I do give you points for creativity, but I don't know why you bothered." *Yes, you do.*

"Just wanted to surprise you."

"Were you going to be in Sacramento anyway?" *No, he'd planned this, just this.*

"I came here specifically to see you." He laid the packet on her desk. "Nice office. A little on the stodgy side."

She didn't take offense since she agreed with his as-

sessment. The firm was old and respected, and the fur-
nishings reflected it in the dark woods and deep-tone
colors. The walls were thick, not allowing voices to
drift down hallways or room to room. "So, Donovan,
what's going on that couldn't wait until I got home?"
I'm glad you couldn't wait.

"The paperwork is done, Laura."

Bells seemed to toll at the statement.

"It's time," he added.

"I'm your lawyer," she said, knowing that was
about to change.

He leaned forward and plucked one of her business
cards out of its brass holder, then set it on her desk right
in front of her. "Which one of these attorneys do you
respect the most?"

Her finger shook just a little as she pointed to a
name. "But he's a partner. All these men are. I think
you'd be happier with Monique Davis. She's an asso-
ciate, like me."

"See if she's available. Please."

Moses came in with a mug of coffee while she made
the call. Donovan set it on a coaster on her desk
without tasting it. He leaned back casually, his body
seeming relaxed, but his eyes were focused directly on
her, his jaw as tight as hers felt.

Over the next interminable minutes, papers were
signed and witnessed. Then when the room was empty
except for the two of them again, Donovan got up and
headed to the door.

She held her breath, stunned. He was leaving? Why? To drag it out further? To wear her down even more with anticipation? To—

He shut the door and walked back toward her, coming around the desk, and setting his hands on her armrests.

"You're fired, Ms. Bannister."

"Good." Everything was simple now. She would know, finally, what it was like with him.

She grabbed his shirt and pulled him closer, but he took the final action. He kissed her, and it was every long-held fantasy come true. His lips were soft and demanding, his tongue gentle and seeking, his breath hot and tempting. She'd been waiting half her life for this moment.

He slipped his arms around her and pulled her out of her chair so that they were body to body, deepening the kiss and contact, groaning, gentleness turning flatteringly fierce. He slid his hands down her back, curved them over her rear, pulled her snugly against him. Sounds came from inside her that she didn't recognize and couldn't control.

"This isn't the place," she said, tipping her head back as he ran his lips and tongue down her throat into the deep V of her blouse.

He touched his forehead to hers, his breath wavering. "Do you need all your girly stuff?"

"Girly…stuff?"

"Yeah. Makeup. Lacy nightgown. You know. Frills."

"As opposed to what?"

"Coming with me right now to a hotel. As is."

Laura was torn. She wanted it to be good. Not perfect—she was realistic, after all, and firsts weren't ever perfect—but good. Memorable. Waiting until they got back to Chance City wouldn't make a difference. Nor would a sexy nightgown. They were both too anxious to deal with the trappings.

"Let's go, newsman. Correspondent."

He chose a large, pricey hotel walking distance from her office, a place big enough to offer some anonymity. Then instead of going to the front desk he guided her to the elevator banks. From his pocket he pulled out a card key.

"You planned," she said as soon as the elevator doors shut. She leaned into him when he put his arm around her and kissed her.

"I hoped." He cupped her face. "I figured the odds were in my favor, but I had to allow room for your feelings about the matter, which I didn't want to presume."

The bell pinged, and the doors opened. They ran down the hall, stumbling, laughing, anticipating. He surprised her by sweeping her into his arms and carrying her inside, her briefcase banging against the doorjamb. She didn't know what he meant by the grand gesture. Maybe nothing. She didn't want to read anything into it.

"You *really* planned," she said, looking around. He'd folded down the bedding, leaving just the bottom sheet, the huge, beckoning expanse of a king bed.

Champagne on ice on the nightstand. Chocolate-covered strawberries. Drapes drawn.

"I'm not a barbarian." He set her down. "Champagne?"

"Later. Much later."

"Laura." He grabbed her hands and held them against his chest. "I have to be home tonight. As much as I'd like to spend the night with you, I can't. Ethan—"

She put her fingers against his mouth. "I understand." She didn't want their relationship to be public, anyway, needing to see where it was going first—if anywhere. For now she just wanted him.

Laura let her suit jacket drift down her arms, then tossed it onto a chair. She stepped out of her high heels, kicking them aside. The rest was up to him.

And he knew exactly what to do and how to do it. How to let the backs of his fingers brush against her skin as he unbuttoned her blouse. How to ease down the zipper of her skirt and slip his hands underneath the fabric to push it to the floor in a bare whisper of sound, her blouse quickly joining the skirt. She didn't wear pantyhose in the summer, so she was left wearing only high-cut white panties and a matching lace bra.

"You have tan lines," he said, surprise in his voice. "So, your story about your bikini being confining was just that? A story? You don't sunbathe in the nude. You just meant to stir me up."

She looped her arms around his neck. "It worked, too, didn't it?"

"Yeah." He kissed her, lingering until she couldn't get enough of him. "The idea of you naked by your pool turned me on, big time. As I'm sure you know. But the tan lines? Very sexy, too."

He took his time then, looking and touching, teasing and promising, her skin on fire from his caresses, from the need. He ran his fingers through her hair, freeing it, finger-combing the tangles out. "You know what people call you?" he asked.

"The Ice Queen?" she guessed.

He looked startled. "Not that I've heard. They call you The Body."

"You mean men. Men call me that."

"Some women probably, too," he said with a grin, reaching for her bra clasp.

She stopped him. "Let's catch you up first." She went to work on him, undressing him as slowly as he'd undressed her, revealing his body to her appreciative eyes and hands. Scars marred his skin here and there, some looking much more serious than others, a visual reminder of the risks he took—*liked* to take. He kept himself in shape, but wasn't overdone. She didn't like the overly brawny look. He was perfect—strong arms, broad shoulders, a wide chest with a dusting of black hair that arrowed straight down his body.

Kneeling, she ran her hands down that tempting line and under his briefs, not rushing the unwrapping, the unmatched pleasure of discovery. She heard him suck air between his teeth as her fingertips grazed his velvety hardness. His thighs went taut; then he hooked his hands under her arms and pulled her up. Her bra was off in an instant, her breasts filling his hands, her nipples sucked into his mouth, teeth scraping, tongue circling. He moved her back until her knees hit the bed and she landed with a bounce. He wasn't slow or gentle removing her panties—nor did she want him to be. She wanted him over her, around her, inside her.

"You are incredible," he said, harsh and low, as he ran a hand down her body, barely touching her, just enough to drive her wild. "Perfect."

She could hardly catch her breath. "So are you." She wrapped her hand around him, guiding him, needing him.

He squeezed his eyes shut for a few moments. "You're on the pill?" he asked, impatient.

I can't get pregnant. "It's taken care of," she said, closing her eyes as he pressed into her, stretching and filling. Then he went motionless, letting their connection just be. She didn't know whether it was her pulse or his she felt—maybe both—but it pounded where they were joined. The absence of movement stretched out the climax she felt building, second by second. He lifted his head and kissed her, hot, wet, openmouthed, mimicking the act itself but not moving his hips, just staying there. She clenched around him.

"Yes," he whispered against her mouth. "Keep going."

He was giving her control, yet he was completely in control, too. Equals. Partners. Light-headed, she tensed and released him rhythmically until his body shook and hers arched. Then at exactly the same moment, they moved in need, melded in desire, soared in satisfaction.

She'd never felt closer to any human being in her life.

And it was perfect.

Too perfect. Scary perfect.

She wrapped her arms around him as he collapsed against her, feeling the sting of tears, and a huge, hot lump in her throat.

How had she ever thought it would be simple?

Chapter Ten

Donovan jammed a pillow against the headboard and tucked his hands behind his head as he waited for Laura to emerge from the bathroom. After all the wondering, the anticipation, and then the incredible pleasure, he should feel relaxed....

He was more tense than ever.

Every reason he'd created for steering clear of her had been valid. She was a banquet, a feast for the eyes and mouth. He should be satisfied, but hunger for her growled, demanding to be fed again. A taste of her wasn't enough.

The door clicked open. He enjoyed watching her walk toward him, but kept his gaze on her face, needing to read what was there. She'd taken a long time in the bathroom, much longer than he would've expected.

Second thoughts, maybe?

No. She would've come out wearing the robe hanging on the back of the door. Instead she was gloriously naked, sexy tan lines and all. Her smile was small and tight. Why? She didn't look as though she'd been crying.

Donovan scooted over, holding out a hand to her, pulling her close, wrapping her in his arms. She let out a long, slow breath and slipped one foot between his.

"Are you okay?" he asked, his breath stirring her hair.

"I'm fine."

She wasn't fine, that much he knew. He needed to see her eyes. "Want some champagne?"

"Sure."

They sat up. He opened the bottle without ceremony and poured two flutes, passing her one, touching the lip of his glass to hers but not saying anything, not sure where he stood. He took comfort in the fact she hadn't gotten dressed.

After they'd each taken a sip, he offered her the plate of chocolate-covered strawberries. He'd had fantasies about feeding them to her, but that didn't seem like something she would enjoy at the moment.

He waited for her to finish eating the first one, then said, "You're quiet."

"I know. I'm sorry."

He was afraid to ask why. "Can we talk about it?"

After a few seconds, she laughed, low and soft.

"That cost you a lot, didn't it? You don't want to talk about it, whatever *it* might be."

"Not really. But I do want to know why you're so quiet." Usually he didn't second-guess anything he did. Maybe other things hadn't mattered as much as this. It was taking every bit of his control not to pull her under him and take her again.

"I'm just feeling a little overwhelmed," she said.

"In what way?"

She brushed his hair, then rubbed his earlobe between her fingers. "You have to understand that this is something I've wanted since I was fourteen—and I didn't even know what I was wanting. Every time you came to town since then, every time I saw you at a wedding or a barbecue or whatever, it was brought home to me again. You've been kind of an obsession."

"And now it's been fulfilled and you're disappointed?"

"On the contrary." She flattened her hand on his chest. "I want more. Lots more."

"I'm willing to accommodate that."

She smiled, then let her hand drift down his chest, his stomach, his abdomen and beyond. "I can see that you are," she said. "It's also complicated now."

He clenched his teeth as her fingertips danced over him. "In what way?"

"The relationship has to be private. Stolen moments. Can you do that?"

It wasn't what he wanted, but he understood what she was saying, and why. There would be too much speculation from his family, putting pressure on them. And then there was Ethan. Donovan didn't want to confuse his son by being gone overnight, and he couldn't invite Laura to stay over at the cabin after they moved in.

But he wasn't giving her up. "I can do that, Laura. Can you?"

She took his champagne flute and set it on the night-stand with hers, then straddled him, settling herself exactly where he wanted her.

"I don't want to give this up, newsman."

"Neither do I."

"Would you be saying the same thing if I were dressed?"

He was glad she'd recovered her sense of humor. "What do you think?"

She took the lead then, and he let himself enjoy the view and the ride. He thought he'd last longer, be able to take more time, use more finesse, but need stopped him from keeping any kind of control—not to mention she kept bringing him to the brink, and then stopping at the pivotal moment. Finally he pulled her down, rolled over and started a rhythm designed to bring them both to climax quickly and mutually again, their bodies and needs attuned.

The moment she hit the peak, he let himself, as well. He thought he'd been satisfied before, but this time went so far beyond it. Sated, maybe. Replete.

Happy.

Now, *there* was a word that hadn't defined him lately.

"Wow," Laura said, her breath hot and shaky against his shoulder.

Which, he decided, summed up how he felt, too.

"Do you want to leave separately?" Laura asked Donovan when they were both dressed and ready to go, their idyll over. Her body ached pleasantly. She wished she could curl up with him and sleep for a while.

"I don't think there's a need for evasive maneuvers," he said, his back to her as he put some tip money on the nightstand.

She heard laughter in his voice. "We're both recognizable around Sacramento, both have had our photos in the newspaper a number of times, our own claims to fame. Local kids make good."

"Tell you what. I won't feel you up in the lobby. How's that?"

She realized how ridiculous she was being. So what if they were seen together? "Dumb, huh?"

"A little." He put his arms around her, but kept her at a distance where they could look at each other. "I imagine it's important to maintain a certain image for your firm."

She toyed with the buttons on his shirt. "My stodgy old firm?"

He smiled. "I said your *office* was stodgy."

"The office reflects the firm." She'd accepted the offer to work for them because she could build a practice quickly there, which had been important to her.

"How long until you make partner?"

"Never. I split my time, so I'm never going to work the eighty hours a week to bring in the necessary revenue to be offered a partnership. They brought me aboard and allowed me to work part-time because of my pageant background, frankly. They didn't say so, but I knew it. They like being able to tell clients that. It gives them a certain cachet."

"Are you okay with not making partner?"

"It's not that I couldn't, because they keep asking me to come aboard full-time. But having my own firm, where no one tells me what to do, satisfies me more than a partnership would. I could work in Chance City full-time if the McCoys would start getting divorces...." She grinned, then kissed him.

He deepened it, then turned it tender, lingering. "I'll walk you to your car," he said finally.

Her automatic refusal of his chivalry didn't come, as she would have expected. After all, it wasn't even dark yet. But some woman she didn't recognize said in her own voice, "Thank you."

They held hands as they walked down the hall and then waited for the elevator, but once inside they let go, standing about a foot apart, each watching the panel of lights as the elevator descended.

They reached the lobby level. The doors opened, re-vealing a man and woman facing away but turning toward them.

Joe and Dixie, Laura realized. What were they—No. Not Joe. Another man with a ponytail.

The color drained from Dixie's face, as it probably had from her own, Laura thought. Donovan recovered first.

"Hey, Dix," he said as he and Laura stepped out of the elevator.

Dixie's face not only regained its color but turned deep pink. "Um, hi." She looked as if she wanted to ask them what they were doing, then thought better of it. Because she would have to explain herself?

"This is Rick Santana," she said without further explanation of who he was. "Rick, these are my friends Laura Bannister and Donovan McCoy."

There was hand-shaking all around, then a moment of awkwardness.

"Rick and I are going upstairs to the restaurant."

"We just came from upstairs ourselves," Donovan said.

"Early dinner?" Dixie asked.

"We met to discuss legal issues."

Laura lifted her briefcase.

"Oh." Dixie leaned over and pressed the up button again. "I'll see you later, I guess."

"Nice to meet you," Laura said to the man. They got on the elevator. As the doors were shutting, Laura made eye contact with Dixie, who mouthed, "I'll call you."

Donovan shoved his hands in his pockets. "Looks like Dixie's finally over Joe."

"Or trying to be."

Their mood turned somber as they left the hotel, not touching, not speaking, the thrill of the past few hours tempered by seeing Dixie out with another man after sixteen years of only seeing her with Joe.

"Are you going to tell your brother?" Laura asked.

"To what purpose? He's already gone from fun-loving Joe to serious Joe, a stranger we hardly recognize. I don't want to see him nose-dive further."

"Maybe it would help him move on."

"Possibly. And now that we've seen her out with someone else, maybe she'll tell Joe, so that he can do the same," Donovan said.

"I'm surprised he hasn't. They broke up, what, about nine months ago?"

"Joe's more complicated than he seems."

It was Friday evening in downtown Sacramento. The streets and sidewalks were bustling. Soon the clubs would be jammed, music reverberating, the dance floors full. She hadn't indulged in the club scene for a long time. Suddenly she wanted to break free of her quiet routine, to have fun, flirting with Donovan the whole time, teasing him, testing her own limits.

But he was a family man now, with responsibilities.

They reached her car in the huge, dark garage under her building.

"Where are you parked?" she asked.

He pointed to a brand-new silver SUV two cars away.

"You bought a car."

"I picked it up this afternoon."

So many questions came to her mind. She asked none of them. He would tell her when he'd made his decisions about his future if he thought she should know. But buying a car seemed to signal…something.

Laura opened her door and tossed her briefcase on the passenger seat. She slid the key in the ignition and then lowered the top. She loved her little red Miata, and since it was a warm evening and her hair was already down and messy, she decided to enjoy the night air.

Then it struck her. "Um, Donovan?"

He slid his hands around her waist. "What?"

"My hair's a mess."

His gaze drifted over her. "A sexy mess."

"Dixie would notice something like that, and not just because she's a hairdresser."

"Meaning, she didn't buy that we were upstairs hashing out some legal business?"

"Exactly."

"What will you tell her?"

"I don't know. But I'll let you know, so you're aware."

"Okay." He pulled her close. "No more wondering," he said into her hair.

"No more wondering. And worth the wait." She felt him relax into her, was surprised it even entered his mind that she wouldn't have felt that way. He always came across as confident.

He kissed her, still tasting of strawberries and chocolate, neither of them having drunk much champagne because they would be driving home. She kissed him back, wishing it didn't have to end.

"Always leave 'em wanting more, hmm?" he said finally, as if reading her mind, something they seemed to do with each other frequently.

She flattened her hands on his chest, could feel his heart thumping, steady and strong. "When will you move into Jake's cabin?"

"Monday or Tuesday. It's going to complicate things for us, isn't it?"

She nodded. He couldn't just walk from his mother's house after Ethan fell asleep. "It's going to take some planning."

"Spontaneity is overrated."

"Says the king of spontaneity," she said with a smile.

"I've learned to adjust quickly."

"Which is the definition of spontaneous, isn't it? I'm a little more routine oriented."

"I've noticed that," he said, pulling her close for a final hug. "Will you consider it too chauvinistic if I follow you home?"

She slid into the car and started the engine. "See if you can keep up, newsman."

He cupped his ears. "What'd you say? Keep it up? I think I've already proven that."

"Show-off."

"Lucky you," he said, backing away. "I'll call you."

She zipped out of her parking space. Because she had a monthly pass instead of needing to stop and pay at the exit gate, she was on her way quickly, but he caught up with her before she got on the freeway. They played cat and mouse the whole trip home, each taking a turn getting ahead, then being behind, neither of them exceeding the speed limit by much. He let her exit first, then followed her home and waited as she parked in her garage. She waved before she shut the door.

Then she was alone. And already lonely.

Chapter Eleven

"Can I honk the horn, Dad?"

"That's not how a gentleman calls on a lady."
Donovan put the car in Park and turned off the engine.
He hadn't called ahead to ask Laura if it was okay to
stop by, but he and Ethan were taking their first drive
together in the new car, and Ethan wanted to show it
off to Laura. "In fact we *should* call first," he said,
pulling out his cell phone.

"She sees us! Hi, Laura!" Ethan unhooked his seat
belt as Laura stepped outside. It was ten o'clock, but
she was still wearing a robe, soft pink and midthigh
length. Her hair was up in a big clip.

She stopped just outside her door. Her newspaper

was a foot away. After a moment she picked it up, then waved in their direction.

"We got a new car!" Ethan shouted. "We came to take you for a ride."

Even from a distance, Donovan saw her tense. He got out of the car and headed toward her, telling Ethan to stay put.

"Sorry," he said quietly, when he reached her. "He's excited. I was just going to call you, and then you opened the door."

She looked incredible, her face makeup free, her hair less than perfect, her nipples pressing at the light fabric. He'd had dreams about her last night. Hot, erotic dreams based on reality now rather than fantasy. He knew what she looked like naked. Knew the sounds she made when she climaxed. Knew how her skin tasted, her own unique fragrance.

"As you can see, I'm not ready to go anywhere."

"You slept in."

She hesitated a beat. "I had a hard time getting to sleep."

"Me, too. You should've called. We could've talked each other to sleep."

"I hope I'm not *that* boring."

"You're—"

"Hey! What about me? I wanna talk, too," Ethan called, leaning out the window.

"He sounds pitiful," Laura said, smiling slightly. "Why don't you let him out of his jail, Dad?"

Donovan whistled, then waved for him to join them. Ethan started to climb out the window. "Stop! Use the door, son." He jogged over, reaching the car as Ethan slid to the running board, and then the sidewalk.

"It's stuck."

Because Donovan had the childproof lock on. He'd forgotten. "You need to wait until I open the door for you."

"Why?" They headed back to see Laura. "I'm a good climber."

"We'll talk about it later," he said as Ethan took off running and threw himself against Laura. Donovan wished he could do the same.

"Please," Ethan was saying, dragging out the word.

"I haven't gotten dressed or even had breakfast yet."

"We can wait for you. I could go for a swim."

"No swim," Donovan said, but otherwise stayed out of it. If Ethan could convince Laura to join them, Donovan would be happy.

"If you're sure you don't mind waiting," Laura said as they all went inside. "Help yourself to anything you find in the kitchen. There's fresh coffee, Donovan."

He poured himself a mug, then a glass of orange juice for Ethan. They went into the backyard, Donovan taking the newspaper with him. He settled Ethan with the only toy in sight, a plastic car that must have been left after the party. Donovan glanced through the paper, something he hadn't done much because the local edition left a lot to be desired. He generally got his news online, needing the broader scope. He'd written a few articles recently, stories he'd been able to gather by phone and Internet; plus, he'd been working on something else that could pay off, in time.

He set the paper aside and sipped his coffee, leaving Ethan to play on his own, something his son rarely did, always wanting company, usually not content to create any games for himself. Donovan had been the opposite as a kid, going off on his own a lot, eavesdropping on conversations in public places, creating stories in his head from what he heard. He loved his family, but he'd craved time alone, although obviously he couldn't remember what he'd been like at age five.

Ethan never wanted to be alone, not even to play in Aggie's family room, which was stuffed to the gills with toys and games. Donovan didn't think his reluctance was only from the upheaval in his life, but a pattern. Anne had probably spent every nonsleeping minute with him. Who could blame her for that?

After a while, Laura emerged, looking cool and fresh in white shorts and a blue T-shirt. She was taking bites of a bagel smeared with cream cheese.

"Are we headed anywhere in particular?" she asked.

He stood, happy to see Ethan putting away the car without being asked. "We have boxes of our things to deliver to Jake's cabin, and some of theirs to bring to the new house. Then we thought we'd head up the mountain a bit. That okay?"

"That's fine." They all piled in the car, Ethan chattering, Donovan totally aware of Laura. He could hear his pulse in his ears, his muscles tightening as memories assaulted him.

"Rides smooth," she said a couple of minutes later, patting the console.

"Yeah," he said, looking her over suggestively. "Best ride I've ever had."

She raised her brows. "Best ever? That must be saying something."

"Laura," Ethan said. "I have my own DVD player. Wanna see?"

"What did we decide about the DVD, Ethan?" Donovan asked, glancing in the mirror long enough to see disappointment settle in his son's eyes.

"Only if the trip is at least an hour long."

"Tough dad," Laura said under her breath.

"Building character."

She laughed then. "Yeah, we'll see who wins this battle."

They pulled into Jake and Keri's driveway and spotted another car parked near the little cabin nestled among oaks and pines.

"Dixie's here," Laura said, sitting up a little straighter.

"Son, you can go on ahead to the house, if you want. Laura and I will catch up in a minute."

"Okay."

Ethan raced across the open space. Dixie came onto the porch and waved at him.

"Are you going to talk to her?" Donovan asked Laura.

"Not here. I expect she'll drop by."

He put a hand over hers. "It was hard not kissing you this morning. And getting harder by the minute."

"You're still referring to kissing?" She wore that sexy smile he loved.

He remembered a moment last night when they'd been lying side by side, facing each other, not talking, and she'd looked like that—content, self-confident and showing a hint of power. Or maybe *knowledge* was a better word; the knowledge that she knew how much she affected him.

He ran a finger down her arm. "Remind me why we're keeping this relationship secret."

Her smile disappeared. "You know every reason, and if you're thinking about ignoring them, this isn't the time or place to discuss it." She grabbed the door handle and climbed out.

He didn't get it. What was wrong with him asking that? They had to be careful around Ethan, of course, but around others? Did it matter?

He watched her for a minute, noting her usually easy stride was stiff and rushed. She stopped as Dixie came down the stairs. They talked briefly before Laura continued up the stairs to the cabin and Dixie headed to her car, without a glance toward Donovan.

"Dix!" he called out, hurrying to join her.

She barely looked at him. "I need to pick up Nana Mae in ten minutes," she said, hooking her purse straps over her shoulder, jangling her keys.

Like Joe, she'd gone from outgoing to restrained since they'd broken up this last time. The two of them used to be the life of whatever party they'd attended, but not anymore.

Was it grief? Were they mourning what they'd lost? Would they heal?

Donovan came up beside her. "I just want you to know that I understand your need to move on. You've been like a sister to me. I want you to be happy."

She tossed her hair, looking like the Dixie of old. "You don't know anything, Donny."

Startled not just by the words but by the harsh tone in which they were delivered, Donovan clamped his jaw. "Feel free to explain."

She shook her head. "I can't. And I'm late." She opened her car door.

"You need to tell Joe," he said. "It'll set him free, too."

She closed her eyes for a few seconds. When she spoke again, her tone held more resignation than harshness. "Joe's always been free. He made sure of it." She got into the car, then looked up at him. "He's just like you and Jake, you know. Except he never left home."

What the hell was that supposed to mean?

He gave up, and headed back to his car. His gaze swept the area, the trees surrounding the property, the cabin set back into a grove. He'd been here uncounted times, yet he'd never noticed how dark it was, and right now it was almost noon in the middle of summer, as good as the light gets.

Jake came across the yard toward him, carrying a large box. "You look...confounded," he said, using one of Nana Mae's favorite words.

"The story of my life these days." Donovan pulled his boxes from the back end of his SUV, opening up space for Jake's to be added.

"I was surprised to see Laura with you and Ethan."

"Ethan's invitation."

"Uh-huh. And you, as the adult, had no say in the matter." Jake hefted a box, waiting for Donovan to do the same.

They walked side by side.

"Nothing to say?" Jake asked.

"Wait until Isabella can sweet-talk you. You'll find it hard to deny her."

"You know, I might've bought that if you hadn't taken so much time to think about it." Jake climbed the stairs.

Donovan followed him into the house, then kept going to the bedroom to stow his box of clothes. The house was so dark that lamps were turned on in every room. He remembered liking Jake's cabin before—it'd felt like a man's place. Which was probably the problem Keri was having with it, and why she wanted to move. It'd been a place for Jake to decompress after a tough security assignment, a job Jake no longer did. And it wasn't a place for a family.

Ethan and I are a family.

He returned to the living room. Ethan was engrossed

in a television program about fishing. Laura held a cooing Isabella.

"I'm thinking it's a really good thing that Laura lives around the corner from us," Keri said to Donovan. "Isabella had been crying for a half hour. Laura walks in? Instant calm. You're free evenings and weekends, I hope, Laura?"

"Send up a smoke signal. I'll be there."

Donovan moved next to Laura and his tiny niece, whose forehead he kissed, her baby scent mingling with Laura's perfume. He straightened slowly, made eye contact with a very serious-looking Laura. She took a few steps back and turned away, making baby noises to Isabella.

Donovan picked up the last packed box from the porch and took it to his car. Jake had already taken care of the rest.

"Do you need these delivered right away?" Donovan asked his brother.

"I don't think so. Why?"

"We're going to take a drive, but I could go back to town and drop the boxes off first, if you want."

"We've got plenty to do in the meantime."

Donovan wished he could talk to Jake about what Dixie had said—that Joe was like them—but he couldn't, not yet, anyway. He wanted to give her time to tell Joe she was dating.

"Everything going okay with Ethan?" Jake asked.

"He's a good kid."

"Are you feeling the connection?"

"Yeah, mostly. He misses his mom—and Millie, too. That makes me feel helpless."

"How much do you think he'll remember of Anne? He seems too young for much to have stuck."

"I'm trying not to let his memory fade. I've been reading up on it, and I know it's an uphill climb. But he'll have photos and videos. That'll help."

They went back to the cabin, Donovan studying it with fresh eyes. Inside, he took one look at Laura and knew she'd rather not go for a ride. He also knew she wouldn't renege, not because of *him* but because Ethan was expecting her to come along.

Suddenly the cabin became a metaphor for what his life had become in the past few years—dark and lonely. Was that what he wanted to bring Ethan into?

"I think we're ready to go," Donovan said.

Laura passed the baby to Keri. Ethan hopped up beside Laura and took her hand. His ease with her tweaked Donovan a little, since Ethan hadn't yet showed much spontaneous physical affection with him. Donovan was very much looking forward to time alone together, to finding the closeness that Ethan had felt with Anne and Millie—and apparently already with Laura.

"Guess what, Laura?" Ethan said. "When I'm five, I'm going to take the training wheels off my bike."

"You are? That's only a couple weeks away."

"I know. I'm very brave, you know. Mum always

said so." His face lost its glow in an instant. "She was sick a long time. I had to be brave." His voice cracked, fading to a whisper.

Donovan ached to hold his son. He met Laura's gaze, could see her dilemma. Ethan had already pressed himself against her, so Donovan gestured for her to go ahead. She knelt. He wrapped his arms around her neck and cried against her shoulder.

"I want my mum. I want her right now."

"I know you do, sweetheart," Laura soothed.

"I don't want her to be in heaven. She needs to be with me!" His heartbreaking sobs tore at Donovan.

Finally he stopped crying, although he kept his face buried against Laura. "I don't wanna go for a ride," came his muffled words.

"We don't have to," Donovan said, crouching behind, laying his hand on Ethan's back.

"I wanna go home."

"That's fine, bud."

"To Maine. I wanna go home to *Maine.*" He finally lifted his head and turned around.

His defiant look caught Donovan off guard. He set his hands at Ethan's waist. "That isn't possible, son."

"Why not?"

Keri handed Laura a tissue, then Ethan. He swiped at his cheeks and nose.

"It's a big trip going to Maine, and it takes planning," Donovan said, weighing his response. "And I think you want to go there because you want to see your mom again, and you know she's not there, Ethan. She can only be in your heart now. But the really good thing about that is that wherever you are, she'll be there, too."

He stared at Donovan for a long time, sniffling. "I hafta go to the bathroom," he said finally.

Donovan kissed his son's forehead, needing that for himself. "Okay."

"I can go by myself." He hurried off, shutting the door, something he didn't usually do.

Donovan dragged a hand down his face.

Laura squeezed his arm. "I know you don't think so now, but that was a good thing that just happened."

"In what possible way?"

"He's comfortable enough to test you. To test his limits with you. It's a *good* sign. He wanted to know if you would get angry, and you didn't."

"I agree," Keri said.

Jake shrugged. "No experience with this, Donny."

"Well, what about when I do get angry? Am I not allowed to correct him when he misbehaves?"

"It's *necessary* that you do," Laura said. "He needs the range of emotion—as long as he always knows you love him."

Donovan looked at the floor, scratching the back of his head. "I can't go just on instinct, can I?"

"To a degree."

"How'd you get to be such an expert?"

"I've watched lots of families relating to each other.

Lots. I've talked to child psychologists and pediatricians. Part of what I do is to counsel people on coping."

The bathroom door opened, and Ethan rushed out as if nothing had happened. "Can we get an ice cream on our drive?" he asked Donovan.

"That can be arranged."

Ethan charged out the front door and down the stairs.

"Mercurial," Jake said. "Look what we have to look forward to, sweetheart." He cupped Isabella's head and half smiled at his wife. Keri laughed.

At least you're not stepping into it five years after she was born. The uncharacteristically sarcastic thought stayed locked in Donovan's head. It wasn't their fault. It wasn't his fault, either. When it came to fault, Anne was—

"Come on!" Ethan yelled from outdoors.

"Oh, Mom offered to babysit Isabella tonight so that Keri and I can go out," Jake said. "We don't want to go too far, so we thought we'd head to the Stompin' Grounds. Want to come?"

"Sure."

"Laura?" Jake asked when Donovan didn't.

"Maybe." She waved and headed out the door.

"I was getting a vibe that you two were together," Jake said.

"Friends," Donovan said, which was both the truth and a lie. The lie part didn't sit well with him, but he was coming to realize that it was for selfish reasons. He wanted to be able to touch her, whether in public or private. "She's been a big help with Ethan, as you can tell. I'll see you tonight."

Outside, Ethan and Laura were crouched down, examining something at the bottom of the stairs.

"Come see," Ethan said. "It's a lizard. He's teeny tiny."

The lizard skittered off before Donovan got to see it. "Lots of creatures live around here, Ethan."

"Like what?"

"Fox and deer. Raccoons. Skunks."

"Skunks! Pee-euw." He skipped ahead as they went to the car, but before he climbed in, Donovan stopped him, put his hands on his shoulders and turned him to face the cabin.

"Does this look like home to you?" Donovan asked.

Ethan twisted around a little to look at his father, his brows furrowed.

Donovan phrased it differently. "Do you think you would be happy living here?"

The boy went still. He looked around again. "You mean, this is where we're going to live?"

Donovan stared back, stunned. He thought Ethan had understood that. Obviously not. "You know Uncle Jake and Aunt Keri and Isabella are moving into their new house. I told you we were going to move into their cabin."

"Oh. I remember now." He paused. "How do I get to Grandma's Aggie's from here?"

"We'll drive."

Ethan shifted his gaze to Laura, who stood beside

them, also looking around as if seeing the property for the first time.

"Can't we walk, Dad? Or I could ride my bike."

"It's a busy, curvy road, not safe for walking or riding."

"And there are lots of creatures."

"Yes, but they're nothing to be afraid of." Donovan crouched in front of his son. "Would you like to live here?"

Ethan hesitated, then finally shook his head.

"Me, either," Donovan said.

Ethan's eyes went wide. "Really?"

"Really."

"Can we live with Laura?"

Donovan didn't dare look at her. "We can't do that, but we can find ourselves someplace with lots of light and a big backyard where you can play."

"Where I can walk to Grandma's? Or ride my bike?"

"You won't be doing that alone for a long time, but yes, we would be much closer."

"Would you buy a house?" Laura asked, her voice tight.

Her face was about as expression free as he'd seen. "We'd rent, for now." He felt the tension in his shoulders ease. Making the right decisions usually resulted in that. "Why don't you and Laura hop in the car, bud? I'll go tell Uncle Jake we won't be moving here."

Ethan threw his arms around Donovan and hugged him hard. Donovan closed his eyes, gathering him close, his hair soft in the cradle of Donovan's palm. He only let go because Ethan squirmed.

Laura's smile was soft and knowing.

When Donovan returned to the car a few minutes later, Jake's understanding words echoing in his mind, Ethan greeted him with "We don't want to go for a drive, Dad. We really, really, really want ice cream."

"Ice cream it is." He started the car, then glanced at the solemn woman seated beside him.

"Are you okay?" she murmured.

He nodded. Or he would be, anyway, as soon as he figured out how to survive the emotional roller-coaster ride that was now his life. At least he'd made one good decision for them as a family unit. That was a step in the right direction.

In town they got their ice-cream cones and sat on a bench outside to watch the Saturday tourist crowd meandering along the wooden sidewalks. After a while they headed to Jake's to drop off the boxes.

"Since we're not going anywhere," Laura said, "how about coming to my house for a swim?"

"Brilliant!"

Donovan gave her a grateful look. "We'll drop you off, go get our suits, then pick up something for lunch later on."

"Sounds good."

He rounded the corner to her street and pulled into her driveway.

"What's that man doing, Dad?" Ethan asked, having

turned around to look at the house directly across from Laura's. "Can I go watch?"

That man was putting up a heavy wooden post. And attached to its crossbeam was a sign—For Rent.

Chapter Twelve

Laura had come *this* close to not showing up at the Stompin' Grounds. At home she'd paced, muttered and stewed. Finally she'd flipped a coin, which led to a second toss, then a third. In a best-four-out-of-seven losing conclusion, she ended up changing into her only Western shirt, black jeans and black leather cowboy boots with pointed toes and a pretty good heel.

As she drove into the parking lot, she didn't see Donovan's new SUV. Maybe he'd decided to skip coming. He'd had a busy day, after all.

She gripped her steering wheel and considered the speed with which everything had happened. They'd walked across the street and talked to the man installing the for-rent sign, Landon Kincaid, who turned out to have graduated from high school with Donovan. They walked through the house, a freshly painted two-bedroom with an upgraded kitchen and bathroom. The yard needed a lot of work, which Landon had intended to do before someone moved in, but Donovan offered, saying he needed a project now that Jake's house was done.

The deal was sealed with a handshake, the keys turned over right then. And starting tomorrow Donovan could stand at his kitchen sink, look outside and see her standing at hers.

Dispatching the image, Laura made her way to the door of the Stompin' Grounds. She hesitated, not wanting to go inside solo, then put her shoulders back and did just that.

She'd been to the bar once years ago and once recently, for a bachelorette party. It hadn't changed in however many years it'd been in business—the same dark-paneled walls, a jukebox churning out country tunes of love and devotion and heartbreak, and beer-sticky tabletops carved with a social minutiae of dates and initials.

She stood just inside the door, letting her eyes adjust to the dark room, counting up the customers. Thirty-two strangers. Then she spotted Dixie sitting at a dark corner table with two other women. Dixie waved her over.

"If I'd known this was your kind of place, I'd have invited you months ago," Dixie said, a twinkle in her eyes, as Laura pulled up a chair, relieved to find someone she knew. Dixie introduced her to the other two women, who decided to go choose some new songs from the jukebox.

"You came alone?" Dixie asked.

"Jake and Keri will be here any time now."

"And Donny?"

"He said so, but it's hard to know for sure. Something could've come up with Ethan." She decided to let Donovan tell Dixie the news about renting the house, although mostly Laura was holding back out of cowardice. Laura knew that Dixie would ask a lot of questions Laura wasn't ready to answer. He'll be within shouting distance? See each other's comings and goings? No privacy?

Not to mention the he's-just-across-the-street fantasizing she would be doing.

Dixie took a sip from her beer as Laura ordered one for herself. She drummed her fingers on the tabletop.

"You want to talk about it?" Laura asked finally.

"About what?"

Laura gave her a look that made Dixie laugh.

"It wasn't a date," they said at the same time, stopped, then grinned.

"You first," Laura offered, not in a hurry herself.

"We really were just having dinner at the hotel. Rick Santana owns Styles."

"The hair salon?"

"He's been a guest lecturer at my school twice this

month. Then he stayed to watch us work and critique it. He's courting me, all right, but for a job in his salon."

Laura leaned forward. "Maybe that's what he told you, Dix, but it's not all he wants. If you could've seen the way he looks at you…"

"I noticed. I was even flattered. But that's it. He's obviously a player. I don't need that."

"Are you going to take the job?"

"The money would be good eventually, since it's one of the most exclusive shops in Sacramento."

The waitress set a beer in front of Laura. She took a sip, wishing for a glass of merlot instead. "Did you factor in the cost of gas and time for the commute?"

"*You* do it."

"Not daily."

Dixie ran a finger around the lip of her mug. "If I took the job, I'd probably move down there."

Shock silenced Laura. Dixie's roots in Chance City ran deep. Her parents owned the hardware store. She had siblings who hadn't left, either, except for brief periods. "I can't imagine you leaving, Dixie."

She shrugged, but Laura could see how much it was costing Dixie to even be thinking about making such a move. Desperate times, desperate measures.

"Your turn," Dixie said in a tone indicating she was done talking about herself. "You can't in any way convince me that you and Donny weren't on a date. I've never seen your hair look like that. I haven't seen you look embarrassed before, either. You are so busted."

Laura had decided that if she ever felt the urge to open up, she would talk to Keri, who was new to town and the McCoy family. But Laura was feeling an affinity with Dixie, and had also come to trust her over the past few months.

"You can't really call it a date. We slept together. That's all. It'd been building for a long time."

"Since high school," Dixie said, nodding. "I remember your obsession."

Laura groaned, burying her face in her hands. "Did everyone know?"

"Pretty much."

"People have been laughing at me all this time?"

"I don't think so. Most seem to be in awe of you, frankly." She put a hand on Laura's arm. "People don't know you. I mean, you've lived here your whole life, and no one really knows much about you, except about your crowns and your job. Everybody loves your mom, but you've always been on a different, I don't know, level? In a different realm? I've wondered for years why you've stayed here."

Sometimes she wondered, too.

Dixie leaned close, lowering her voice. "Are you gonna do it again with Donny?"

"The first opportunity I get."

"You intend to keep the affair secret?"

"Yes."

"Okay. Then I will, too."

Dixie's friends returned, and the conversation

changed to gossip and speculation. Laura sipped her beer, surreptitiously checked out the front door every time it opened and thought about Donovan. Yes, she wanted to continue to sleep with him. But a new wrinkle was complicating that decision. She'd been almost in love with him for years—she'd acknowledged that to herself finally. But today she'd fallen deeper when he'd talked to Ethan about his mother, and then when he'd brought Ethan into the decision about moving into the cabin. Now she not only loved Donovan, she also respected and admired him. And wanted him. She'd never felt that for one man before, not all those things at one time.

Donovan was a born father, and that was the big complication. Without a doubt, he would want more children. All three of the McCoy brothers had been known as the men who wouldn't commit, but recently that label had been altered some. Jake had done a one-eighty and now was a devoted husband and father. Donovan had made a seamless transition to fatherhood himself. Laura had no doubt that Joe would follow in their footsteps. She'd watched him with his nieces and nephews for years, the easy way he had with kids and how well they related to him.

But as for her and Donovan having a future? It wasn't in the cards she'd been dealt. She just needed to get him out of her system now, while she had the chance, so that she could move on. She would find a way to fall out of love with him—not an easy thing but doable. People did it every day. She saw it in her practice all the time.

The front door opened, and in walked Jake, followed by Donovan and then Joe.

"Keri's not with them," Laura said, worried.

"It can't be anything serious or Jake wouldn't be here," Dixie said, having gone very still when Joe appeared.

Jake said something to his brothers, then crossed the room toward her and Dixie.

"Everything's fine," he said right away. "Isabella was fussy, and new mama couldn't bear to leave her. She put her foot on my butt, shoved me out the door and ordered me to have fun."

"Which means you'll have one beer and be gone," Laura said.

He grinned. "Probably not even that since I'll be driving. Anyway, I knew you'd be wondering." He walked off to join his brothers at the bar.

And while she couldn't see Donovan's eyes from so far away, she interpreted his body language just fine, making her wish she'd tossed the coin a few more times, enough times to grant her own wish to stay home and let him come to her instead.

Keeping her hands off him tonight would be a character-building experience.

Beers in hand, the brothers headed for a table. Donovan maneuvered himself into a chair where Laura was in his direct line of sight. She hadn't stood up yet, but he figured the view was going to be spectacular. He couldn't recall seeing her in jeans before, which seemed odd, jeans being the American uniform. Maybe it was a sign she was loosening up.

"Can we talk about Dad?" Joe said. "The other day, you two were wondering if he was happy. Why would you think he wasn't?"

Donovan had been giving the subject a lot of thought, too, since it'd first come up. "He never went anywhere but to work and home. Or an occasional trip to Sacramento or Tahoe or Reno, maybe. Can you remember taking any vacations?"

"With eight kids? Vacations cost too much." Joe sounded defensive. "He raised us and provided for us. I'm sure that's all he expected of himself. But we did lots as a family. We just stayed close to home."

"Maybe *you* did," Jake said. "You were the baby, so there were fewer kids to deal with as time went by, and more money. Mind you, I'm not criticizing. It was a great childhood." He looked at Donovan. "Do you think people have to leave home to be happy?"

"It seems like seeing the world a little would help you appreciate home even more. He wasn't even in the military." Donovan was still trying to figure out what Dixie meant when she'd said Joe was just like Jake and him, except he hadn't left home. "You haven't gone anywhere, Joe. Are you okay with that?"

"Doesn't matter, does it? I have a thriving business I can't leave."

"You also took over the man-of-the-family role when Dad died, and you were the only male offspring living here. You were stuck. But did you want to leave? Do you now?"

"I think about it." He took a good, long drink.

Donovan exchanged a look with Jake. Joe wasn't a complainer. In many ways he reminded Donovan of their father. He went off to his job every morning without griping about it, worked hard and had seemed okay with his life—until recently. Maybe the breakup with Dixie wasn't the only thing that had changed him.

"And if I decide to do something about it, I'll let you know, okay?" Joe said. "I may be the youngest, but I'm no kid." He stood. "I'm gonna say hi to some friends."

"Methinks he doth protest too much," Jake said when he'd gone.

"Yeah." Donovan watched Joe pull up a chair at a table with two women. Dixie turned away and focused on Laura, laughing as if she was having a great time.

"Despite what you said this afternoon, I know you're not just friends," Jake said, gesturing with his head toward Laura. "You can't stop looking at her."

"Hell, Jake. Even you said you'd been tempted through the years."

"I was joking. She's always only had eyes for you."

Why was it others seemed to know that but not him? Except for that time in high school, she hadn't come on to him again. And there'd been plenty of opportunities.

"You're stuck, aren't you?" Jake asked, humor in his voice.

"In what way?"

"You want to ask her to dance, but you can't—for whatever reason you think is valid. And you can't ask Dixie, because Joe would retaliate by asking one of the women he's sitting with. The potential for fireworks tonight is more than any Fourth of July celebration."

"And you sit there smirking, because you've got a wife and you're done playing the mating game."

"Damn straight. If I'd known marriage would bring such peace to my life, I would've done it years ago."

Peace. Was that what had been missing in his life? He recalled how reluctant he'd been to leave town this last time, how he'd stalled until the last moment—and that stall had resulted in his meeting his son, instead of being called back home by someone in his family. Plus, it hadn't even been a big deal to him that he was postponing an important article, the kind he usually craved researching and writing, his lifeblood. It should've been a big deal.

Peace. He wouldn't call his relationship with Laura peaceful. Arousing, frustrating, satisfying in some ways, yes. But not peaceful. And secret. He exposed secrets for a living. Was that why hiding the relationship wasn't sitting well with him?

And now he would be living across the street. They hadn't had a moment in private to talk about it, and he figured she must have plenty to say.

He studied her from across the room. She threw back her head and laughed at something Dixie said. He hadn't seen her laugh like that before. She was generally more subtle with him. He wanted to know the side of her that let go and laughed so boisterously.

"I dare you," Jake said, elbowing his brother.

"To do what?"

"Ask her to dance."

"She warned me she had two left feet. I verified it."

"So don't move much." Jake was laughing. "Never known you to be a coward, Donny."

Jake was right. Not only was Donovan being cowardly, he was also hesitant, something new for him. He decided to accept the dare. Several couples were on the small dance floor. They wouldn't be in a solo spotlight.

He stopped at the jukebox and punched in a song to follow the one currently playing. He zeroed in on her as he crossed the room. She glanced his way, looked back at Dixie, then did a quick double take when she realized he was heading directly to her. She ran her hands down her thighs.

He stopped next to her chair. "Evening, ladies."

"Hi, Donovan," Dixie said, her eyes twinkling.

She knew he and Laura had slept together, he thought, seeing pure sass in her expression.

"Do you know my friends Sheryl and Nancy?"

"I don't." He shook hands with each of them. "Can I buy you all a pitcher?"

"Well, sure," Dixie said. "That'd be nice."

He signaled the bartender, then turned to Laura. "May I have this dance?"

She fiddled with her napkin, shredding it. "You know I don't dance."

"It isn't a two-step, Laura. We'll take it slow."

He wasn't used to her not speaking her mind, and it was pretty evident that she wanted to have words with him. He put out his hand, counting on the fact that she would rather go with him than have to explain to the others why she wouldn't.

She stood, resistance in her stance.

Donovan did his best not to gloat.

Chapter Thirteen

Laura hadn't figured she'd ever have a second dance
with Donovan. In some ways it felt even more important than sleeping with him, because it was public.
Sure, lots of people who weren't lovers danced, but she
could always recognize the difference. People who
were intimate allowed the other person into their
personal space comfortably. And it felt completely
natural to be in his arms, even if she was furious at him.
Even if she couldn't dance well.

"You're ticked," he said, sliding an arm around her
waist, drawing her close but not too close.

"How could you do this? We agreed to keep our relationship to ourselves."

"Look around. No one cares what we're doing."

She did look around. "You're wrong. Several people are watching us."

"In the same way that they're watching everyone else who's dancing. Look, Laura, I've been thinking about this all day. What would it hurt if people knew we were seeing each other? I'm not talking about spending the night if Ethan's around, but in general."

Because it's going to end. The thought hurt, but it was the only truth she knew.

"I don't like lies," he said before she responded.

"We haven't lied to anyone."

"A fine point, and you know it. It's a secret. Secrets always involve lies. In my line of work, I uncover lies."

"This isn't about your job."

"True. It's about *me.* My integrity. And yours. Anne kept Ethan a secret from me. I will never forgive her for that. Never. And you can't convince me that a secret has less consequence than a lie. Either one is a deal breaker for me."

"I see your point." The point being, she'd been keeping her secret from him all along, when she'd always been honest with every other man she'd dated—semihonest. She didn't divulge the details, only that she didn't want to get married or have children. She hadn't told Donovan, and she didn't know why. Well, maybe she did. But now she'd sealed her fate with him by keeping the secret from him. She should come clean…

But she didn't want to give him up. Not yet.

"But," she added, finally breaking her silence, feeling him tense. "It's still new. Let's see for ourselves where it goes before we involve anyone else."

"I can see we need a little more discussion about this before you agree with me." He sort of smiled and pulled her a little closer. "Enough talk about that. Let's enjoy our rare opportunity to dance. It's the only time I get to lead, you know."

She was more than willing to abandon the serious topics, but she wasn't sure dancing was going to solve anything. "That's because I don't know how to dance."

"Exactly. You're damn good at everything else. It's my turn to show off."

She had just begun to relax when the song came to an end. Grateful, she started to pull away. He tightened his hold as a new song began, the lyrics far too appropriate as Toby Keith sang about kissing—and getting lost on the dance floor. She didn't want to get lost. She wanted to keep her head about her.

"So. We're going to be neighbors," she said, trying to ignore the song.

He smiled, slow and sexy. "Life can change in the blink of an eye, can't it?"

"I guess you know that better than most people." She'd slept with him. She already knew what his body felt like, skin to skin. Yet dancing, fully dressed, had her just as revved up as being naked in bed with him.

"I guess I do." His fingertips pressed into her lower

back, something no one else would be able to see but that she could feel, heat expanding from that point.

Her head was spinning, just as the song said. "You've got a lot of work ahead, cleaning up that backyard."

"I'm always up for a challenge."

She had a feeling they weren't talking about the same thing, her feeling confirmed when he eased her close enough that their hips aligned. "Will you install play equipment?" she asked.

"It came already installed—thirty-three years ago." He flattened her other hand against his chest so that he now had both arms around her waist. "Works perfectly, as you know. Takes you soaring. Safe, too."

She couldn't look at him anymore, at the knowledge in his eyes and the anticipation of more. She shifted a little, touched her head to his cheek, looking over his shoulder. The action brought her breasts against his chest. He drew a long, slow breath.

"What will you do about furniture?" she asked, pointedly redirecting the conversation with what little remained of sane thought.

"There are these interesting places, counselor, called stores. If you haven't seen one before, I'll be happy to show you. They even let you test out mattresses. Decide whether soft works for you. Or maybe you like hard better."

She gave up trying to keep the conversation nonsexual. "I like both—for entirely different reasons."

"Really? You enjoy soft?"

"For what it implies. There's the breath-catching aftermath. And the anticipation of what could happen again. And don't forget the fascinating process of transformation."

"Ah. The adjustable mattress. I've heard of them."

"How about you? What do you prefer?"

"The kind you can sink into." He spun her around and around, matching the lyrics.

She felt dizzy but didn't stumble. It was a different kind of dizzy. One that had her leaning back, staring at his mouth. "Donovan…"

He bent low, brushed his lips against hers, an electrifying touch. She kissed him back, needing him…

Laura jerked back. What was she doing?

The song ended. She pulled herself free. "I knew this was a mistake," she said low and fierce. "Don't make a scene, okay? I'm going to leave now."

"I won't make a scene. But you don't need to leave."

Oh, yes, she did. And right now, before she made a fool of herself.

She said goodbye to Dixie, grabbed her purse and left. By the time she got in her car, she was shaking. He had a way of making her forget herself. She'd always been able to stay in control, except with him. And now everyone there had witnessed that. She'd kissed him. In public.

She fumbled with her key, trying to get it into the ignition, when her passenger door opened, and Donovan climbed in. "I need a ride," he said lightly. "I can walk to Mom's from your house."

She looked over her shoulder. "Your car is right there."

"I've been drinking."

Like her, he'd had time to drink half a glass. She turned back and stared out the windshield, swallowing hard. He was being thoughtful, not wanting her to drive when she was so upset.

"Do you want me to drive?" he asked quietly.

It was the quiet, understanding way he asked that had her nodding. Without speaking they got out, then traded places. She was angry, but more at herself for allowing herself to be in that public situation with him.

He started the engine. "I've been wanting to take your car for a test spin."

She latched onto the chance to change the subject. "You should've asked. I would've let you. It's just a car."

"No car is ever 'just a car,'" he said, backing out.

"You mean you wouldn't let me drive yours?"

"Maybe. After the new-car smell wears off."

"How long does that take?"

"About five years."

She laughed, still shaky but settling down. "I'll bet you don't keep a car that long." She tossed her head, the wind lifting her hair as they drove along the highway.

"If that turns out to be the case, I'll let you drive it once before I trade it in."

His palm rested on the gearshift. He could easily slide his hand over an inch or two and set it on her thigh. The fact that he could, even if he didn't, turned her on. And they weren't in public anymore.

"This is a great little car," he said. "Not stodgy at all."

"It's how I balance myself with my work."

"You balance it just fine without doing anything."

"So, you don't find me stodgy?"

"Depends on whether you're naked or dressed."

"Really? You find me stodgy when I'm naked?"

He shot her a look, then realized she was joking. "The librarian—or maybe in this case, the lady-lawyer—fantasy is popular for a reason."

"Hmm. Interesting."

He took the turn to her street. She pulled a remote from the glove box and opened the garage. He eased the car in and shut it off.

"Thank you," she said simply.

He dropped the keys in her hand. "Anytime." When she didn't say anything else, he started to open the car door. She hit the remote to close the garage door.

"Would you like to come in?" she asked.

The garage door touched ground. "Seems like you already answered that question for me."

"You know where the front door is."

He slipped a hand behind her head and pulled her toward him to kiss, something she'd been aching for him to do all day when they were together with Ethan and again then since he'd walked into the bar. Need sparked greater need, creating fire that crackled and flared between them.

The garage still held the day's heat, was stuffy and stifling.

"Let's go inside," he said.

"I thought you'd never ask."

Chapter Fourteen

By the time she opened her door and got out, Donovan was there, kissing her again, tasting her welcoming warmth, feeling the vibration of her moans transfer to him, rousing, tempting. They found their way into the house. She flattened her hands on his chest and pushed away slightly.

"I'll be back," she said, breathing hard. "I have to do something."

Birth control, he decided, shoving his hands through his hair. A diaphragm, maybe? They hadn't discussed it last night except that she'd said she'd taken care of it.

"Hurry," he said, impatient.

She disappeared down the hall into her bedroom.

Aroused and eager, he made his way to the living room. In almost no time he heard her door click open. She came down the hallway toward him, holding a few casebooks, her hair up, a pair of reading glasses on and wearing a white bra, panties and a skinny black tie.

Lady-lawyer fantasy. He knew enough of the legal lingo to say, "Looks like I've won my appeal. Habeas corpus, counselor." She did, indeed, "have the body."

She laughed as she continued moseying toward him, her hips swaying. He popped the snaps of his shirt, dragged it free of his jeans and hurled it toward the couch.

"Need help with your boots, newsman?"

He dropped onto the sofa and raised his foot. Leaning over him, she pulled one boot off, her breasts barely contained by her bra, her nipples hard and inviting behind the lace; then she turned around, settled his other boot between her thighs. He planted his other foot on her rear, while she yanked off the second boot. He wanted to tell her how exciting she was, how different, but he figured she'd take that as a comparison. No one wanted to be compared.

He stood. The rest of his clothes joined his shirt on the sofa, spilling like a Dali painting, looking as surreal as he felt. He'd been worried that they wouldn't repeat what they'd done last night, had figured she would find some way to stop the relationship in its tracks.

He was glad to be wrong.

"Shall we go sequester ourselves in my bedroom?" she asked, letting her hand glide down his torso, then wrap around him.

"Obviously, the evidence needs no oral argument," he said, drawing in a breath. "Although you can give that a shot, too."

She laughed, soft and sultry. "Let's go present our cases. Maybe we'll create a few precedents of our own."

She'd yanked the bedding off, as he had done at the hotel, except that his had been deliberate and neat. He was glad she'd been in such a hurry.

They fell onto the bed together, wrapped each other up in a tangle of arms and legs, then just stopped and held on, both breathing heavily and haltingly. After a minute he pulled back slightly and kissed her tenderly, remembering how upset she'd been earlier, wanting to make sure she knew he cared about her, that she wasn't just someone to have sex with. And vice versa.

"You are a constant surprise," he said against her lips as he got rid of her undergarments.

"Good." She deepened the kiss, indicating she didn't want to talk anymore.

But he always accepted challenges. "You're a lot more fun than you let on."

"I'm not laughing now, newsman."

He did laugh then, but at the same time cupped her breast, circling the nipple with his thumb, then sliding down her to taste the hard flesh. She arched, offering herself as he took his time exploring the landscape of her incredible body, drifting lower and lower, savoring her, enjoying every sound, every movement. He sent his hands on a journey, gliding and stroking, cherishing and arousing. Only when he was ready to give in to her increasingly demanding pleas did he let his mouth take over for his hands, enjoying her, appreciating all of the woman she was. Finally she gripped his hair and rose up, her pleasure and satisfaction audible, giving him a memory to cherish, too.

She came down slowly, breathing hard, her skin damp and hot, and then she went limp against the mattress, sprawled out, eyes closed.

He leaned on an elbow next to her. "What's the verdict?" he asked. As if he didn't know….

"Nolo contendere." She wasn't contesting it. She opened her eyes, ran a finger across his lips and smiled in that sexy way she had. "But I haven't made my closing argument yet."

He flopped onto his back. "I await your rendering."

She straddled him, her hair brushing his sensitive skin as she treated him to the reverence of her seeking hands, her tender lips, the swirl of her tongue over and around him. Her fingertips went on journeys of discovery, making promises of fulfillment, but delaying and delaying until he couldn't stand it a second longer. She finally let him find that elusive satisfaction, gifting him with incredible, amazing pleasure. Then he fell against the bed much as she had, limp, his needs quenched.

Later, when they were lying side by side recovering and he was contemplating round two, her phone rang. She let it ring. Her answering machine was turned up loud enough that they could hear the message being left.

"This is Jake McCoy. I'm sorry to bother you, Laura, but I'm looking for Donovan. If you see or hear from him, please tell him he's needed at home. It's not a medical emergency or anything, but Ethan needs some reassurance. Thanks."

Donovan and Laura looked at each other. "He probably had a nightmare," he said.

"Whatever the reason, you need to be with him," she said, rolling toward him and touching his shoulder.

He kissed her, softly, pulling back reluctantly. He wanted to ask if she felt better now, if she'd recovered from what had happened at the Stompin' Grounds, but it wasn't the way he wanted the night to end.

"I'll drive you," she said, getting out of bed when he did. "I can drop you off a block away."

He started to refuse, then didn't. It would save him ten minutes—and give him ten more minutes with her.

He dressed in the living room, where he'd left his clothes. Pulling his cell phone from his pocket, he saw that he'd missed two messages, one from Jake, one from his mother.

"Ready?" Laura asked from the door leading to the garage.

No. "Yes."

She handed him a brush.

They didn't kiss goodnight when she dropped him off. They just stared at each other for a few seconds. "I'll call you," he said, leaning back into the car.

"This has to stay private, Donovan. We had good reasons when this started. Nothing's changed."

He had no time to argue. She left, her taillights disappearing into the night as he climbed to his mother's porch. Inside the house, Ethan sat in Aggie's lap, his face tear streaked.

"Where *were* you?" he cried, resisting Donovan's efforts to take him from his grandmother.

"I explained that you went somewhere with your brothers," Aggie said, but she was silently questioning why he hadn't been with Jake and Joe.

He reminded himself that his son wasn't completely comfortable with him yet, and that Ethan was used to being with women, including a mother who'd been too sick to leave the house for as long as Ethan could probably remember. His grief was fresh and raw.

"I'm here now, son," he said quietly, rubbing Ethan's back. "C'mere, please."

At first Donovan thought Ethan would reject him, but he flung himself into Donovan's arms instead.

"Just don't go, okay? Don't leave me!"

Donovan carried him outside and sat in the rocking chair, the still-warm night quiet enough to hear the crickets. He rocked his son for the first time in his life, tucking him close, breathing the scent that was distinctly Ethan.

"I know this has been a big change for you," he said softly. "I know you miss your mom and Grammy, and the life you used to have. And I know you're a little worried about how different everything is. But the thing is, I can't promise to stay with you all the time. I need to go to work again soon. You'll go to school. I also need to go out sometimes with friends, just like you'll have sleepovers with Grandma Aggie or other people. You'll make friends at school."

He tightened his hold on Ethan. "But when we're apart, it will only be for a period of time." He wished he could assure his son that he would always come back, but it wasn't a promise he could make—just as Anne couldn't. "You'll always be with someone you want to be with, someone who loves you. Someone we both trust. Okay?"

Ethan drew a deep, shaky breath. "I was scared. I woke up and you weren't home."

"I'll tell you what. From now on, I'll tell you if I'll be going out, even if you're already going to be asleep before I leave. Is that a deal?"

Ethan was quiet for a long time before he finally nodded.

"All better now?" Donovan asked.

"I need ice cream."

"Oh, you *need* ice cream."

Ethan giggled. "Yes, I need it."

"All right. I'll join you."

Crisis averted, Donovan thought, relieved. "Run in and wash your face and hands. I'll fix two bowls. And one for Grandma, if she wants." She'd disappeared, so he wasn't sure if she'd gone to bed.

As Ethan skipped into the bathroom, Donovan dialed Laura.

"He's okay," he said when she answered, her hello soothing. "Abridged version is that he woke up and got scared because I wasn't here."

"Thank you for letting me know."

"We're going to have ice cream."

"The perfect cure-all."

He heard the smile in her voice. "Thanks again for tonight."

"We both know you were the one deserving of thanks. I appreciate your coming to my rescue, newsman. For noticing I needed rescue. Even though I didn't think so at the time. I'm a little used to controlling situations."

She would've been fine, but he was glad she saw it the way she did. "And my thanks to you for bringing one of my fantasies to life," he said, a clear image of her dressed like a lady lawyer glaring like neon in his mind.

"That actually was my pleasure, too. Good night, Donovan."

He snapped his phone shut, then tapped it against his thigh. Within the next couple of days, he and Ethan would move into a house and start their life as a family. And soon he would have to figure out what to do about work, a decision he'd put off for good reasons, but that he couldn't put off for much longer.

But all that could wait until he'd had a bowl of ice cream with his son.

Chapter Fifteen

"I can have a crew here and clear this yard in half a day," Joe said the next morning, standing next to Donovan on the back patio.

"What fun would that be?" Donovan peeled his T-shirt over his head as he watched Ethan drag a shovel through the foot-tall weeds, making motor sounds with his mouth.

"Fun? I don't get it, Donny. You're renting. Why put in the effort?"

"Because it's something I can work on with Ethan."

"Ah. Okay. That makes sense. So, what would you like me to do, aside from loaning you tools?"

"If you could help with the hauling, that would be

great. You've already put in extra time lately on Jake's place."

"Limited time. Keri wants to do her own thing. Anyway, what are brothers for?" He elbowed Donovan. "You'll let me choose the plants, right? And tell you where to plant them?"

His brother knew him well. "Yeah. Landon said he'd pay for them, within reason."

"Lucky him. He'll get my wholesale cost, so you can load up this place."

"Hey, Dad!" Ethan shouted from the far end of the yard, a good forty feet away. "Can we get a dog?"

"Nope."

"Why not?"

"Landlord's rules. No pets."

"Aw, man." He picked up the shovel again and started zigzagging around the yard.

"Is that true?" Joe asked.

"No idea. Didn't ask." He recalled the speech he'd given Laura the night before, and figured this lie might come back to haunt him sometime. Then he justified it by not knowing whether he was lying or telling the truth. He just didn't wanted to break Ethan's heart.

And he wasn't ready to commit to owning a dog.

Joe took a sip of his coffee, then said casually, "I'm gathering I had to drive your car home last night because you went off with Laura."

This was exactly the situation Donovan wanted to

avoid. Should he lie to his brother now, too? No. To hell with it.

"Yeah. I apologize for not asking you. I needed to catch her in a hurry."

"So Jake told me when he gave me your keys. I understand the attraction, Donny. In fact, I've seen it coming for years."

"But?"

"But watching you two on the dance floor? I know I'm not the king of relationships, but yours didn't look comfortable."

Donovan considered that, and decided Joe was wrong. In private it was comfortable much of the time, exciting much of the time and also frustrating much of the time. He could talk to her more easily than anyone else, even his brothers, with whom he shared the most.

"Appearances are deceiving," Donovan said, swiping a pair of gloves from the ground and grabbing a shovel.

"There's an original choice of words."

He laughed. "I'm out of practice."

"Uh-huh. About that. What's your plan?"

"Still not sure. I'd like to have it figured out by the time Ethan starts kindergarten, which gives me about three and a half weeks. It's hard to believe he's only been here for a couple of weeks." And it'd only been a couple of days since he'd first slept with Laura, yet it felt as if they'd been together for a long time.

"Anybody home?" someone called out.

"Speak of the devil," Donovan said at the sound of Laura's voice from inside the house.

"Not really," Joe said, looking at Donovan oddly.

"It's just a figure of speech, Joe."

"I know what it is, but you weren't talking about Laura." Joe grinned. "I guess Ethan starting school wasn't what was really on your mind, after all."

Laura came through the open sliding glass door, her mother behind her. Donovan almost went to Laura, almost embraced her. She looked temptingly beautiful in a cool blue summer dress and sandals, her hair up, which always brought more attention to her pretty hazel eyes and her elegance, in general.

"Good morning," she said. "I hope you don't mind us just dropping in. Mom wanted to see the place."

"Hi, sugar," Dolly said, her red hair shimmering in the sunlight.

"Welcome, sweet 'ums."

"I think I'm missing something," Laura said, looking from Donovan to her mother in question.

"Inside joke," Dolly said, patting Donovan's arm.

"Laura! Dolly!" Ethan raced over. "Come see my bedroom."

"I saw it yesterday, Ethan," Laura said. "I'm sure my mom would love to, though."

"Lead the way, young sir."

He giggled and took her hand in his grubby one, dragging her into the house. Joe excused himself to get more tools from his truck out front.

"When my mom isn't working for me, she's an interior designer, did you know that?" Laura asked.

He took a couple of steps toward her. "How are you this morning, counselor?"

It took her a few seconds to refocus. She smiled. "I'm good, thank you. Did you sleep well?"

"Surprisingly well." He dragged his fingers down her bare arm, enjoying how her skin rose in bumps. "Did you?"

"I had very pleasant dreams."

"I didn't." He bent close to her ear. "I had dreams that would shock you."

"Spinning new fantasies for me, newsman?"

He liked how she returned his heated look. "Don't you have a few of your own?"

"I might." She ran a pink-polished fingernail down his chest, tracing the line that disappeared into his jeans, then hooking the edge of fabric and pulling him near.

Donovan grabbed a handful of her hair and squeezed. Her touch was feather-light. He lowered his head. She rose toward him—

A loud clatter had them jumping apart.

"More tools," Joe said before striding out the gate again.

"He knows about us," Donovan told Laura, who had put a little distance between them. "He guessed, and I decided not to lie about it. But he'll also keep his mouth shut."

She nodded, which could mean just about anything.

"Dolly says I can decorate my room with fish," Ethan announced when he and Dolly returned.

"Fish?"

"As a theme," she said. "He said he likes to fish."

Donovan wasn't aware Ethan had ever been fishing, but a kid-size fishing pole would make a good birthday gift. "Okay."

"If you'd like help with the decorating, I'd be glad to, Donovan."

"I wasn't planning on getting much new, except mattresses. Until I know for sure what the future holds, I'm just accepting all donations."

"Do you have a style?"

"Early McCoy," Joe said, returning, pushing a rototiller. "It's too bad all that stuff from the Widow Braeburn's house already sold."

"Right," Donovan said. "Because the spindly-legged tables and prim little love seats would've looked great here in the man house."

"Man house?" Laura asked.

"'Cause we're men," Ethan said, then high-fived his dad.

"I can still help," Dolly said. "I do staging for sales all the time. I'm good at it. Just have everyone put their donations in the garage. I'll take it from there."

"Ethan and I get veto power, though, okay? We don't want frills or doilies or knickknacks, right, bud?"

"Right." He frowned. "What's doilies?"

"Something we don't want. Not manly."

Ethan puffed up. "Right."

"It's a cute little place," Dolly said. "Won't take much to fill it up. As for the backyard—good luck."

"It'll be great, you'll see." He looked around the space, envisioning it finished. "Yards like this are just begging to be filled up with kids."

Silence fell like a heavy quilt. Even the birdsong stopped.

"We have to go," Laura said briskly. "We have reservations for brunch."

Donovan saw her exchange a look with an obviously surprised Dolly. Laura was lying. Why?

"Drop by anytime, neighbor," he said as evenly as possible when what he wanted was to sit her down and make her tell him why she'd lied. "And, Dolly? I'll take you up on your offer, thanks. See you later, Laura."

"Bye. So long, Ethan. Have fun."

"I will!"

They left through the side gate. He would've picked apart everything that had happened except that all of a sudden his yard teemed with people—sisters, brothers-in-law, nephews, even a couple of nieces. He tried to stop them, but none of them paid any attention.

Which was the price one paid for being a McCoy— a pushy support system that ignored your requests when it decided you were wrong.

Well, maybe help cleaning out the yard wouldn't be so bad. He and Ethan could do the planting themselves, and perhaps install a small jungle gym or swing set. There would be enough projects for the two of them to do together.

And he was counting on Ethan inviting Laura over a lot. At least there was one McCoy male she couldn't seem to say no to.

"So, in order to turn a lie into the truth, we have to go eat a second brunch?" Dolly asked as she and Laura got into the Miata and headed to Dolly's house. "Because I couldn't possibly do that, no matter how much I love Honey's blueberry pancakes."

"I'm sorry I put you on the spot. I just wanted to get away."

"I know, sweetie." Dolly patted Laura's hand as she put the car in Reverse and backed out of her driveway. "You're in love with him."

"Yes."

"Wow. No hedging at all. This is serious."

"Semiserious." Laura turned the corner and headed for her mother's house, a few blocks away. "Because it just can't be, you know?"

"Do I?"

"Of course you do. You heard him yourself. He wants to fill the yard with kids."

"I heard him. I also saw the way he looked at you. You haven't told him, I gather."

Laura shook her head. She pulled into her mother's driveway. They went into Dolly's house, a charming little cottage that showcased her extraordinary talent

with paint and fabric. Summer roses from her garden
filled vases in every room, the fragrance filling the air
until she opened the windows, releasing the heat.

"Iced tea?" Dolly asked.

"Sure." She followed her mother into the kitchen.
The tea would be home brewed and peach flavored, the
goblets cut crystal.

They took their glasses and sat inside a screened
sunroom off the back door, the view of the rose garden peaceful.

"So," Dolly said. "Talk."

Laura swallowed. "I hardly know where to start."

"Maybe I will, then. I've got a few questions myself."

Relief spread through her. "Okay."

"Did you honestly think you could be with him and
not fall in love? He's been your one-and-only for most
of your life, even when you've been with someone else."

"Yes, I thought I could. I figured it would help get
him out of my system. Maybe I was naive. Maybe I
was rationalizing. When it came down to it, I couldn't
pass up the opportunity."

"And now you're in deep. Too deep to recover?"

"Everyone recovers, Mom. Eventually. You got over
Dad, right?"

Dolly looked away, took a sip of her iced tea. "Sure."

Laura went still. "You're lying."

"I'm not, sweetie. I was just remembering. I got
over him, but it took years, and him getting married to
someone else."

A sandbag seemed to have dropped onto Laura's lap. "You never told me."

"I was furious. Then devastated. I had to put him out of my head."

Laura could barely breathe. "Did he have more children? Do I have siblings?"

"I don't know. I can tell you where he's living, if you want to find out for yourself. He lets me know when he moves."

"Why?"

She shrugged. "After the first note, I stopped opening them. But I have them in a file, and you're welcome to have them, if you want."

"Why is this the first time I'm hearing about it, Mom?"

"You never asked."

Laura fixed her gaze on her mother.

"Oh, all right. I didn't want you to get hurt anymore. He walked out without looking back. If he had regrets later, he could've come here and made amends. I never moved, would never have denied him the chance to see you." Dolly squeezed Laura's hand. "I thought he was my soul mate. I loved him with all my heart. But love wasn't enough. It really never is, no matter how much people spout otherwise. And it's certainly not enough when it's one-sided."

"Why did he marry you?"

Her mother's smile was crooked. "I guess you're old enough to know now. Because of you, sweetie."

"You were pregnant?" Too many revelations at once had Laura's head spinning.

"Four months."

"Why didn't I ever know about this?"

"What purpose would it have served?"

Laura couldn't believe she hadn't heard it at some point through the years, especially during high school, when teenagers sometimes took great pleasure in revealing others' dirty laundry. "It's part of my history, Mom."

"Mothers do what we can to protect our young."

"You act like you're a mama bear and I'm your cub, needing to be kept safe from predators. I haven't been in need of protection for a long time."

"I thought about telling you when you graduated and became an adult, more as a cautionary tale, so that you wouldn't make the same mistakes I did. Then you got sick. You had a hard enough row to hoe then."

Laura decided she could waste time and energy being angry at her mother for keeping such a secret—or just get past it. She chose the gentler path. "Do you regret it? Having me? Making your way in the world solo?"

"Not one bit. Not one single bit. I could've married again. I had opportunities and even a few marriage proposals, frankly. But I think you learned how to build a wall around your emotions because I did, too. I'm sorry for that."

"You denied yourself the possibility of happiness."

"My life is far from over, you know. I'm only forty-

nine—an age you'll find yourself before you know it."
Dolly leaned toward Laura. "Does he love you?"

"He hasn't said so. More important, we want different things, Mom. He hasn't figured out his own life yet. I'm not sure he's going to be around much."

"He won't leave Ethan alone for long periods."

"I don't think he has a choice. He's in the top tier, and he thrives on it. He'll want to set an example for Ethan, too—that you should do what you love. I figure he'll take off more time than he used to, but that's it."

"Well, you know him better than I do."

They went quiet for a long while. Laura couldn't go home, not without being seen, and she needed some time alone. Needed to cocoon.

She'd known it was going to be hard, having him living across the street. She just hadn't realized it was going to be impossible.

Chapter Sixteen

"Where the hell are you? The Giants' ballpark?"

Even with all the noise surrounding him, Donovan recognized the *NewsView* executive editor's voice over his cell phone. "Close," Donovan said. "My mom's backyard. My son's birthday party. What's up?"

Rupert Cole liked to brag that he'd discovered Donovan, who'd decided years ago to let Rupert think that. It never hurt to be an editor's favorite.

"How do you like the sound of Special Projects Editor?"

Donovan walked away from the party, going out the side gate and onto the front porch, sensing that this phone call was going to be one of the most momentous of his life. "How do I like it for what?"

"For the job of a lifetime."

"Are you making me an offer?"

"Yeah. One you can't refuse."

Donovan sat on the stoop of his mother's house. He knew all the titles at *NewsView*. Special Projects Editor wasn't one of them. "You created a job for me?"

"You got it."

"Why?"

"Because we want to keep you."

"What makes you think you wouldn't?"

"Gimme a break, D. You have no interest in going overseas for months at a time anymore. Or maybe even days. Tell me I'm wrong."

He couldn't—but he hadn't known for sure until Rupert just said it, making it real.

"Right," his wise editor continued when Donovan said nothing. "So, here's the deal. Special Projects Editor. You get to run your own show, and you'll answer only to me. You'll work out of the bureau here in D.C. I think the salary will make you happy. Plus, you'll have benefits. Profit sharing. Stability. That's what you want most, right? For you and Ethan?"

Benefits. Stability. Not the edge-of-the-cliff life of before, but a grown-up job. Calling his own shots. A chance to own a home. A steady income. Excellent schools for his son. Donovan already had a wide circle of friends and contacts in D.C.

"When do you need an answer, Rupert?"

"Schools here start in three weeks."

Three weeks. And in Chance City, ten days. Ethan was already registered. They'd walked the campus, checking it out, had peered into the kindergarten class-room, analyzed the playground equipment for the level of fun and challenge.

"I appreciate this more than I can say," Donovan told his editor. "I need to tell you that I've got some-thing else in the works."

"I heard." He chuckled. "It's a small world, our world. I don't have a problem with you pursuing that at the same time."

It was more than he could've hoped for—but was it an offer he couldn't refuse? "I'll get back to you. Thanks, Rupert. Not just for the job offer, but for what it represents, too. I appreciate the confidence."

"You've earned it, D. I'll e-mail you more details. Figure you're interested in how much we think you're worth. I know it won't be as exciting as being in the field, but being in charge should help. I'll be home the rest of the weekend, if you want to talk."

Donovan slid the phone into his pocket but contin-ued to sit on the stair, aware of the party noise from the back side of the house, but not ready to face it yet.

"Donovan?"

Laura stood in front of him. He hadn't heard her approach.

"We're about ready for the piñata."

He straightened. "Yeah, okay. Thanks."

"Is everything okay?"

He ran his hands along his thighs, then stood. "Maybe. Any chance I can come by later and talk to you about it?"

"Of course."

"It'll have to be after Ethan goes to bed. I'll ask one of my nieces to babysit."

"That's fine."

He returned to the backyard with her, aware of her curiosity. Aware of her, period. As he always was. They'd had little time together the past couple of weeks. It had been more complicated than he'd thought, living across the street. He knew when she came and went. He saw her in the kitchen. Saw when her lights went out at night, wishing he could join her.

The days she worked in Sacramento now, she stayed until dark, something new. Ethan was already in bed when she drove in.

The house was too quiet when his son was sleeping. Donovan had gotten used to people coming in and out all the time at his mom's house. He'd never expected to miss that.

He and Laura had slept together only twice since he'd moved into the house, both times rushed, both times physically satisfying but vaguely unsatisfying, too. She'd seemed a little distant, and he'd started to feel uncomfortable with the…arrangement. He couldn't call it a relationship, since they still hadn't gone public with it. He didn't like the hiding.

But maybe it'd been the right thing to do, after all. It could make leaving easier, not just on them but also

Ethan, since he didn't have a clue about how Donovan and Laura felt about each other.

He stopped in his tracks. Did *he* even know how they felt about each other?

"You're scaring me," Laura said, her gaze intense.

"I apologize." People were looking at them—his brothers, his mom. Nana Mae. He hadn't yet followed through on his promise to take his grandmother to lunch. She wouldn't let him off the hook too much longer. "Everything's all right, Laura."

She walked away, sat between Dixie and Keri again, and Donovan made himself get back into the spirit of the celebration. Ethan had met three other five-year-olds recently, who were now waiting their turn to hit the piñata. He was settling in, making friends. How could Donovan take him away from that?

For the job of a lifetime? How could you not?

As Joe handled the piñata portion of the party, Donovan lingered in the background. He knew why he'd left Chance City all those years ago. He'd had good reason, a calling, and a need to fulfill it. He'd done that, could continue to, probably at even greater success and fame. And personal satisfaction, something he'd gloried in.

He could admit that now. He'd reveled in his success. Anne had been right—he'd been driven by his career, to the detraction of all else. He'd set a course and stayed on it, picking up speed year by year.

And what do you have to show for it?

Plenty. Success beyond his dreams. He'd been places most people never went, experienced firsthand what most never would. And he was only thirty-three years old. He still had a lifetime of such experiences ahead of him.

At what cost?

He studied his son, who was laughing uproariously as he tried to hit the piñata blindfolded. A mere month ago he'd been shy and cautious. He would've needed Donovan by his side, holding his hand.

Or Laura.

Donovan's gaze slid to her. Her eyes sparkled as she watched Ethan. She leaned closer to Dixie now and then to comment, but her gaze never strayed from his son.

She fit. She was surrounded by McCoys like a fine wine amid longneck bottles of beer. But she fit. He'd seen her go up to his mom today and give her a hug, something she wouldn't have done a month ago. Like Ethan, she'd settled in.

So have you.

Yes. So had he.

Donovan made his way to where his grandmother sat, enjoying the festivities. "I'm wondering what your calendar is like?" he asked, crouching beside her. "Do you have time for lunch this week?"

"As a matter of fact, I'm free tomorrow, after church."

"I'll pick you up at noon. We can take a drive up to Tahoe, have lunch, play the nickel slots a little."

Before her stroke a couple of years ago, she'd loved that kind of day.

"Let's just go to the Lode. It was sweet of you to offer, Donny, but I don't have the energy for anything more than that."

It was the first time she'd admitted it to him. She generally resisted any hint that she'd slowed down. How many years did she have left? She was eighty-nine. She had every right to take it easy.

"I'm fine," she said, patting his cheek. "Don't look so worried."

He'd observed the fragility of life so many times, in so many places. In the middle of a war there was no time to contemplate it. But here, where his life had begun and with his grandmother sitting beside him, aging minute by minute, he thought about it. She was becoming more fragile day by day, but only in body. In spirit she was as strong as ever, maybe stronger. Her perspective on his situation would be different, clearer.

"I love you," he said, kissing her cheek.

"Oh, my sweet boy!" She framed his face, her eyes glistening. "You always were the one to surprise me the most. And not always in a good way," she added with a laugh. "I love you, too."

His gut unclenched. He patted her shoulder and moved next to Jake, who happened to be standing behind Keri, and therefore close to Laura. He held Isabella, was swaying a little, bouncing a little.

Donovan studied his niece, her eyes drifting shut, then popping open at the sound of the stick hitting the piñata or people cheering.

"Could I take over?" he asked his brother. A couple of months ago, Jake had set Isabella in Donovan's hands, but he'd given her back almost instantly, unsure.

Jake didn't hesitate. He transferred his daughter to Donovan's arms. She stared at her uncle, serious and intent, then suddenly smiled, transforming her beautiful little face. His heart melted.

"There's nothing like it," Jake said.

"I missed this part of the dad experience." Another reason not to forgive Anne.

Laura twisted around to face him. "You look very natural," she said, a smile on her lips but not in her eyes.

Isabella slept finally as they finished up with the piñata, then throughout the opening of the gifts.

"Last one," Aggie said, carrying a large, flat, rectangular package. "The card says Ethan and Donovan."

"Come on, Dad! Help me open it."

Donovan passed the soundly sleeping Isabella back to Jake, then joined Ethan, who'd plucked the envelope from the package and handed it to Donovan.

"It's from Laura," Donovan said, reading the card.

"I already got a present from Laura." A pair of shields, encrusted in plastic gems, matching the swords from before.

"I guess she thinks you need two."

Ethan just grinned.

They peeled off the paper together, revealing a framed canvas painting of father and son. Oohs and aahs followed.

"Look, Dad! It's us!"

Donovan swallowed hard. Them, indeed, looking like a matched set, each of them wearing blue shirts, their heads touching, beaming with the same smile. He remembered that day in the park, had forgotten Laura had taken photographs. She'd had this one turned into a portrait, a tangible memory.

"Thank you," he managed to say to her. They might as well have been alone, because she was the only person he saw. "It's perfect."

"I'm glad you like it. Mom painted it."

The McCoy circle had expanded even more with the addition of Dolly, who'd spent most of the day talking with Aggie, as if they were old friends. Maybe they were. Donovan didn't know.

He sat back and looked around. This was his tribe. His village. His people.

His family.

"Have you had a good day?" he asked his son.

"The best." Ethan hugged him, long and hard, something he'd learned from his Grandma Aggie, Donovan figured.

"Me, too," Donovan said.

But was it enough? He was itching for more in his life, something the new job could provide. The backyard at his rental was finished, but the lawn too new and tender to host a family party yet, which was why they were at Aggie's. The fact that he'd even considered throwing a party still surprised him.

Aggie started singing "Happy Birthday," everyone joining in right away. Five candles were lit on the chocolate-cake-with-chocolate-frosting request from the birthday boy, who grinned from ear to ear.

If Donovan turned down the job, Ethan could grow up here, where he wouldn't have the global experiences of living in D.C., but where he was already loved and accepted. That trade-off for Ethan would be fine.

The question was, would it be fine for Donovan?

Chapter Seventeen

Laura climbed out of her pool and grabbed a towel, burying her face in it. She'd swum lap after lap after lap, had stopped counting how many. Her arms ached. Her hips and thighs swore at her.

Outside the French doors to her bedroom, she stripped off her suit, wrapped up in her towel and went inside. Nine-thirty, the clock said. An hour she'd been out there churning out laps. A full hour.

Compensating for the birthday cake and ice cream….

No. Countering a whirlwind of emotion.

Something was on the horizon for Donovan. Something crucial.

He'd called earlier, saying he'd be over around ten.

She still had time to shower, blow-dry her hair, put on a silk negligee she'd just bought. They usually didn't have time to set a romantic scene. She wanted to give him a memory—and herself, too, because she didn't know how many more opportunities there would be.

At precisely ten o'clock came a soft tap on the front door. Laura shook her hair back, more nervous than she could remember. And it *was* nerves, not anticipation that had her hands trembling and her breath shaky. It had to be nerves.

She opened the door. He didn't say anything, didn't have to. Desire flared in his eyes, in the hardness of his jaw, in his posture. He slipped inside, locked the door and pulled her into his arms, kissing her with a ferocity she returned in full measure. She wasn't interested in tender any more than he was.

He backed her against the foyer wall, attacked her mouth with his, hot, wet and deep, his throat vibrating with needy sounds. He squeezed her breasts, tugged at the straps of her negligee, dragging them down to savor her flesh, his tongue leading the way, nipping with his teeth, sucking her nipples into his mouth. He kept going, lower and lower, her gown pooling at her feet, his hands flattening her hips to the wall as he cherished her, stealing her breath, scattering all thoughts, leaving only sensation, rising, powerful sensation. She skyrocketed, soaring higher and higher until bursts of color shot through her with such force she had to brace herself.

Before she'd even come down all the way, he lifted

her, her legs wrapped around him, and carried her down the hall to her bedroom, dropping her on the bed. His shorts fell away. He didn't bother with his shirt, just plunged into her and drove hard, his face contorted as he moved rhythmically.

"Come with me," he murmured, slipping a hand between their bodies, dipping his fingers low, stroking her with incredible softness, considering his own need.

She slammed into a hard, fast climax that startled her with its intensity. He joined her, his body as hard as marble, his groans primal and flattering.

He said her name, low, almost painfully. She wrapped him in her arms and held him, wanting to soothe. He didn't move. Didn't roll off her, but lingered, his weight on his elbows but still heavy against her body, and exactly where he was meant to be.

"If I'd known you like negligees that much," she said when she couldn't stand the silence any longer, "I would've worn one sooner."

He lifted his head, kissed her gently, making no joke in return.

"What's wrong, Donovan?"

He finally moved away, pulling off his shirt, then settling down beside her. "Nothing's wrong. In fact, a case could be made for saying something's amazingly right."

"Are you going to tease me all night?"

He tucked a strand of her hair behind her ear. "That would be a first, wouldn't it? We've never had 'all night.'"

No, they never had. Never more than a few hours at a time. She'd come to resent that in ways that surprised her. "If you don't tell me right now what's going on, I'm leaving this bed."

He grabbed her hand, keeping her there. "I never expected we'd have this conversation naked," he said, smiling for the first time.

This conversation? Alarms blared in her head. Even before he started talking, she knew it would be about his work. Then he did talk, confirming it. And what an extraordinary job offer—life offer, really, because it would change his life forever. And Ethan's.

"When are you leaving?" she asked, wishing for the protection of clothes.

"I haven't accepted the job, Laura. I haven't even come close to it."

"How can you not? You know what your chances are of having another opportunity like this. Really, Donovan, how can you not take the job?"

"Because there are other things to take into consideration. Like Ethan."

She waited for him to add, "Like you," but he didn't.

She wanted to be done with the conversation. Wanted to give in to that bright ball of pain building inside her. She couldn't do that in front of him.

"What do you want from me?" she asked. "What's my role here?"

He moved back a couple of inches. "I'm thinking out loud so that you can help me see every angle."

She couldn't deal with it naked anymore, so she got out of bed and went into her closet, coming out wearing a robe. He'd pulled on his shorts and T-shirt and was sitting against the headboard, looking…distant.

Laura sat on the bed, facing him. "Ethan will grow where he's planted. You've already witnessed that. It only matters that you be together, and that his father is happy and fulfilled. That's all he needs."

He frowned. "I expected you to talk me out of it."

"I don't think you did. I think you came to me for honesty." She was glad now that she hadn't told him her secret, that she could continue to keep it. She could go back to her life as it was, which was just fine. Give her a few months—or years—and she would be fine, anyway.

"Actually, I've been dealing with something similar," she continued. "The partners are pushing me hard to come on board full-time. They've decided part-time no longer works for their purposes."

"What are you going to do?"

"I'm seriously considering it. It's not like the people of Chance City couldn't drive to Sacramento to consult with me." Except many would be priced out of it, probably, considering that her hourly rate in Sacramento was almost double what she charged here in town.

"But you told me you'd have to be working eighty-hour weeks," he said. "Add your commute, and you won't have a minute for yourself."

"I'd move to Sacramento." She figured she could buy a house or condo, and if Dixie decided to take her own job offer in Sacramento, too, they could share until she had the resources to go out on her own. It might be fun having a roommate, a true girlfriend. Laura had kept herself private for too long, far too long.

"Move to…? Are you serious? You said you'd have a full-time practice here, if you could make a living at it."

His memory was too good. "Well, I've rethought it. Like your offer, it's tempting."

He stared at her for a long time, a usually successful technique, she knew, for getting someone to say more. She didn't add anything. Couldn't add anything. Because any second now, she was going to break down and sob on his shoulder, pleading for him not to go, pleading for him to love her back.

She couldn't do that to him. They had no future. He wanted more babies, a real family life. She would even move to D.C. with him, if he asked, if she thought they could make a go of it, that he wouldn't eventually resent her for not giving him more babies. He'd made enough comments lately that she knew the inevitable.

"So," he said finally. "You'd be okay with me leaving?"

"I've had a great time with you. And you know I adore Ethan." That bright ball of pain was reaching epic proportions. If he didn't leave soon… "But, Donovan, you have an incredible talent. It shouldn't be wasted."

"And it wouldn't matter to you if I left?" he asked again.

I love you. "Do what you need to do."

"You didn't answer the question."

"Your decision has to be based on what's best for you and Ethan."

His gaze was steady. She looked right back.

He reached for her hands, held them in his, still staring at her. She thought she would spontaneously combust, so intense was the fire inside her. She wanted him with all her heart and soul, wanted him in sickness and health, for better or worse. Until death do them part.

She wanted to be a mother to Ethan, to watch him grow, to help raise him to be a man. Ethan was her only hope for that, because she would never give in to her emotions like this again.

"You're right," Donovan said finally, breaking a long silence. "You're right most of the time, you know?"

She shook her head, a lump in her throat preventing speech.

"I should go," he said.

She walked with him to the front door, her hand in his. He kissed her, thoroughly but without heat, the tenderness almost unbearable. Then he was gone.

One hand covering her mouth, one pressed to her stomach, she ran to her bedroom, fell facedown on the bed and gave in to everything she felt, all the pain, all the longing, all the love.

Maybe if she'd been honest with him from the beginning, it would've made a difference. Maybe. Regardless, she'd waited too long, had been too afraid that

it would be the deal breaker for them. So she'd taken
what she could from him, promising herself no regrets.

Which was the biggest lie she'd ever told herself.
She was going to regret his loss for the rest of her life.
Of that she had no doubt.

Donovan didn't sleep. He tried, several times, but
he always wound up sitting in a chair on the back patio.
If he'd been a list maker, he would've done the pros
and cons, but there were too many factors to weigh, too
many lists to compile and cross-check with others.

In the end, he would have to go with his gut.

By the time he picked up Nana Mae at noon and
they were settled in their booth at the Lode, he was no
closer to making a decision than when he'd gotten
Rupert's call yesterday.

He didn't bring up the job offer while they ate, just
kept the conversation light, getting her to reminisce
about her life, asking questions he hadn't been interested in before, grateful she was still alive when he'd
reached an age where he was genuinely curious about
her history.

He noticed other things, as well. How elegantly she
ate, using each utensil precisely, reminding him of the
etiquette lessons she'd given all her grandchildren.
He'd gone out into the world prepared to be tested over
a meal by potential employers, heads of state, four-star
generals or women on dates, knowing he could pass
any test of manners with flying colors, not only

because he knew which fork to use when, but how to converse, how to put people at ease.

She'd done that for him, for all of his siblings. He loved her, but even more, he respected and admired her.

When they were finished with their sandwiches and salads, Honey brought hot lemon tea and pound cake for Nana Mae, her traditional finish to any meal at the Lode.

"You drink too much of that stuff," she said to Donovan as Honey refilled his coffee mug. "Moderation in all things."

"Bores me."

Her eyes twinkled. "I know."

"Not likely to change, either."

"I know that, too. So, what's the real reason you invited me to lunch?"

He leaned toward her, remembering at the last minute not to put his elbows on the table. "I've been offered a job at *NewsView,* a full-time, permanent, regular-paycheck-and-benefits, big-challenge job."

"And the *but* is?"

"It's in D.C."

She nodded thoughtfully. "What are you going to do?"

"I don't know yet."

She took a careful sip of her tea, her way of gathering her thoughts. "Your father once had an offer like that."

Donovan sat back, surprised. "He did?"

"Not the same as yours, of course, but an offer that

would've suited him, a chance to leave town, be independent, see the world. He was twenty-one. He and Aggie had been dating about eight months."

"Mom would've been seventeen."

"That's right. They'd known each other for years, but when she started her senior year, he took notice of her in an entirely new way. She was so different from him, you know? Outgoing, bubbly, cheerful. She's the same now, just more mature, of course. I could see why he fell for her. He'd been too serious all his life. She brightened his world in ways I can't even describe.

"Then along came this job offer just as he was about to propose, the day of her high-school graduation. He came to me, wanting advice. I told him then what I'm going to tell you now, Donny. You need to do what makes you happy. If you're not happy, no one around you will be. It all may seem complicated, but it's really quite simple."

Donovan had figured that his grandmother would talk him into staying in Chance City. If he'd given it more thought, he would've realized she wouldn't do that. His mother might, but not Nana Mae, which was probably why he was talking to her and not his mom. "Dad didn't take the job."

"He did not."

"Did he regret it?"

"You grew up with him. What do you think?"

His father had remained a quiet man, dependable, patient and consistent. But he'd loved his wife openly, lovingly, their affection public, if subtle on his part. "He seemed content," Donovan said. "But if he had regrets, we never would've heard about it."

"Yes, you would, Donny. Not directly, but he would've been telling you one way or the other all your life. And if he were here today, he would tell you to check with your heart first before you make a decision, not your head. Not your practical side, but your selfish side. And once you've made a decision, don't look back. Don't regret. Have no remorse. Keep moving forward."

A hot lump settled in Donovan's throat. "Mom and Dad were incredible role models. I always knew I wouldn't settle for less than what they had."

Which was why he'd never asked Anne to marry him, even though he'd thought he'd loved her. If he'd loved her enough, he would've sacrificed for her, and he didn't. She must've known....

Nana Mae patted his hand. "You'll make the right decision. Whatever you decide will be right, because it'll be for the right reasons. Let your walls collapse for a while. See what's behind them."

Walls. The word triggered a memory of his conversation with Dolly. What had she said? That Laura had put up some pretty solid walls.

Why?

He hadn't asked why, hadn't gotten deep enough into her head to know why she'd built walls, why she'd needed them in the first place. Last night, he'd seen her pull back from him. She'd encouraged him to take the job, to go all the way across the country—for a job. She hadn't expressed any hope that he wouldn't go—not in words or even in her eyes.

Why? She'd said, too, that Ethan would bloom where he was planted—even though Donovan knew she loved Ethan, knew she loved being with him, and he with her.

And why was it so important to Donovan that she wanted him—and Ethan—to stay?

"You just made a decision," his grandmother said, watching him.

"I checked with my heart, like you said. It made it for me, loud and clear." He captured her hand across the table. "Thank you. Maybe I would've come to the same conclusion, made the same decision, but I would've probably suffered for days trying to make it. You made it simple. You couldn't have given better advice."

"When it comes down to it, Donny, most things in life are simple."

But not people. People were complicated and complex, with walls built around emotions and old hurts. You could chip away at them or shatter them all at once with a wrecking ball.

And there wasn't time to chip away at Laura's walls.

Chapter Eighteen

Laura left her hand cradled on the telephone receiver after ending the call, one that had taken her a week to work up the nerve to make. She didn't know how she felt yet except—

Her doorbell rang. Through the peephole she saw Donovan staring right back at her, waving, smiling.

He'd made a decision.

She drew a steadying breath, then opened the door. "Hi."

His smile went away. "What's wrong? You're pale."

She choked up a little, wanted to throw herself in his arms and let him hold her. She clenched her fists instead. "I just talked to my father. Come in."

He did, but stood just inside the front door, not trying to lead her into the living room, but cupping her elbows, steadying her.

"Did he finally track you down?" he asked.

"I called him. Turns out my mom has known all along where he lives—Orlando." She swallowed. "I have a brother and a sister. Twins. They just graduated from college. He—my father—wants to see me. He wants forgiveness."

"What are you going to do?"

"You know, given what I do for a living, I've seen how easy it is for people to become estranged and not know how to fix it, even when they desperately want to. I'm willing to give it a shot. It won't be easy, but I want to try. In some ways, I need to forgive my mom, too, for keeping his existence a secret from me. I'm in the mood to forgive." There were more important things in life, she'd decided, than holding grudges.

"I forgave Anne," Donovan said.

The short, simple sentence filled the entire room with significance. "I'm glad. How'd you come to it?"

"By realizing I hadn't done my share in the relationship. That I was at fault, too. She was wrong not to tell me I had a son, but it's done and can't be changed. I want a clean slate."

Laura's blood ran cold. She couldn't move. "So you've decided to take the job."

He cocked his head. "That's an interesting conclusion you've jumped to, counselor."

She would miss that, him calling her counselor in that playful way.

"Let's go for a walk," he said.

"Where?"

"Not far. Come on, Laura. Be spontaneous with me."

"Bully," she said, his dare a tempting one.

"Whatever works."

She grabbed her keys and left the house with him on what was probably the hottest day of the summer so far.

"One of the things I thought about during my sleepless night last night," he said as they walked, not holding hands, but occasionally bumping arms, "was your decision to move to Sacramento and take on an eighty-hour-a-week job. I wondered what had changed during the past few weeks, because I didn't get the impression that was something you wanted to do. So the only answer I could come up with was that you'd gone into self-protection mode. More important—into sacrifice mode. You wanted me to leave here with the knowledge that you, too, were moving on to something bigger. Your life would go on without me."

"You say in all humility." She didn't like that he could figure her out so well, so easily. *Yes, you do. You like it a lot.* Her heart was doing the talking now, instead of her head. No one else had ever read her so well.

He smiled gently. "I understand you. Is that so bad?"

"What do you think you know?"

"I'll tell you in a minute."

They rounded a corner and kept walking toward the park. She could usually summon up a great deal of patience, but not today. Not now. She wanted to get this over with. She especially didn't want to walk by the house. *Her* house, as she always thought of it. The place where life could be perfect, where a family could be made—and a wonderful life.

"Ever been inside this place?" Donovan asked, pointing to the house. Her house.

She shook her head.

He held up a key. "Let's take a look."

"How…?" She stopped the question cold, because she didn't really need to know how he'd gotten the key, but rather how he'd known that this was the house. Her house.

They went inside. She saw peeling paint, water-damaged hardwood floors, a filthy stone fireplace. She also saw beauty and warmth, peace and fun, which echoed through the house like their footsteps as they walked from room to room, checking out each of the five bedrooms, three bathrooms, unusable kitchen and gorgeous sunroom.

Donovan stayed uncharacteristically quiet, as if they were visiting a shrine. Maybe they were. Her own shrine to family and dreams that she'd given up on twelve years ago.

Finally he leaned against a pillar in the sun room. Still he hadn't touched her. She needed so much to be touched, to be held. The house, her house, was calling to her, as it always had, making promises she knew couldn't be fulfilled.

And somehow she knew Donovan was about to make things harder on her.

"I know you do need a partnership offered to you, Laura, and I'm here to do just that," he said, his voice sounding strange after the long silence. "There's a catch, however."

"Isn't there always?"

"How'd you get to be so cynical?" he asked, smiling slightly but not waiting for an answer. "The catch is, this partnership would require more than eighty hours a week. Also, the revenue can't be counted in cash, but it's immeasurable, refilling itself to overflowing all the time. Marry me, Laura. Live here with me. I love you."

He loved her? The room spun, not just with joy but worry. "But—"

He pressed his fingers to her lips. "No buts. Just love me and my son, and whatever other children we're blessed with."

How could the best day of her life also be the worst? "Children," she repeated.

"Yeah. I'm not talking a dozen or anything, but a couple more. I didn't realize how much I'd wanted kids until Ethan came along. This house could hold just the right number, don't you think?"

"You're not accepting the job offer?"

"I'm not. When I asked myself if I wanted the job

of a lifetime or the chance of a lifetime, it was a simple choice. I've been out in the world. I know the value of life, the importance of love, the necessity of a true partnership. I could have all that in D.C., too, if you were willing to move there. But this is where I want to raise my children—with you. I've learned that nothing is forever, that life constantly shifts and changes. I *can* go home again."

She walked away from him, staring at the overgrown backyard. He didn't give her time or space, but was beside her in an instant.

"Yes? No? Maybe? Give me time? Drop dead? Not if you were the last man on earth?" he said, covering anxiety with humor.

"I've been keeping something from you, Donovan. Something important. No, more than that. Something critical."

"I'm listening."

"I didn't tell you in the beginning, because I thought this would be temporary."

"This?"

"Us. Our affair." The word sounded harsh in her ears. Affair. It really was what they'd had, but it sounded tawdry now, especially knowing she loved him—and he loved her. She'd ignored that declaration, not letting him see how much his words had meant to her. It was what she'd wanted—and feared—would happen.

"Our affair," he repeated. "Is that how you see what we've had? No emotions involved, just sex?"

"I can't have children." There. She'd said it. Now they could deal with it.

He waited a few beats. "How do you know that?"

"Because twelve years ago, I had uterine cancer. I had a hysterectomy, then chemotherapy and radiation, all of which saved my life, but took away my ability to have children."

She felt him staring at her, but she didn't make eye contact, continuing to look out the window, seeing nothing. He turned away.

She trembled from keeping herself so still, so rigid. She wished he would just go, get it over with, let her get on with the healing she would need to do. Go to D.C., she wanted to scream. Get out of my life. Take your adorable son with you.

After what seemed like an hour, he faced her, took her shoulders and made her look at him. His eyes were wet. "Cancer."

She nodded.

"You could've died," he said, low and hoarse.

He pulled her against him so hard she bounced off him a little, held her so hard she could barely breathe. That she'd started crying didn't help.

"You could've died," he said again.

"I didn't," she said, comforting him, running her hands over his back, up into his hair, as he pressed his face into her shoulder. "I'm here."

He kissed her, emotion spilling from him. If she'd had any doubts that he loved her, they were gone now.

His fear, his relief, all poured out of him in that kiss that was tender and grateful and life-affirming.

"Why didn't you think you could tell me?" he asked, touching his forehead to hers.

"My reasons were purely selfish. I'd wanted you for so long. I finally had a chance. I didn't want to give you up until I had to. When you turned me down in the high-school parking lot, I was devastated. I wanted a memory this time."

He finally straightened. She brushed his cheeks with her hands, as he did hers, both of them smiling a little.

"You know why I turned you down, don't you?" he asked.

"You said I was too young."

"I also told you I was leaving. Believe me, I was more than tempted. But what kind of man gets involved with a woman when he knows he's going to leave?"

The silence that dropped between them was palpable.

"Yes," he said, without her asking the question. "Yes, I must have already decided I wouldn't be leaving Chance City when we first slept together. I didn't know it consciously, but I must have known, because that's not the way I operate. And you haven't answered my question, Laura."

She believed he loved her. Still, a big issue needed to be addressed. "You said you wanted to fill your yard with kids."

"You're too literal, counselor. What makes you think I wouldn't be open to adoption? Or if that's not right for you, we borrow the neighbors' kids or my nieces and nephews from time to time. But can you imagine the number of children I've seen who've been orphaned? How many kids I wished I could take home and keep safe? Are you willing to do that? Adopt?"

"Yes," she said instantly, the word scraping along her throat. "I never saw myself as a mother, never allowed it, but I've learned I have a lot to give a child, especially when I love his father."

"So that's a yes, you'll marry me?"

"That's about the biggest yes in the history of the world."

He kissed her, softly, sweetly, then framed her face and asked, "Aren't you curious about how I'm going to support us?"

"Yes, I am, in fact, although I have to tell you that you'd better come up with something good, because I'm quitting the firm in Sacramento. My income's dropping by a whole lot. We may not be able to afford this house."

The thought of not having this house now that she'd come to believe it was hers struck fear in her.

"Relax. We can afford this house," he said right away, reading her expression perfectly. "Remember last month when you were giving me ideas about work I might do that would allow me to stay here with Ethan? Well, it seems a publisher wouldn't mind paying me to write fiction, based on my experiences. I'm going to create a series starring an ace journalist who makes a name for himself by going where the story is, risking his life for it, no holds barred, and the enemies he makes."

"Will he ever fall in love and settle down?"

"What? Turn him into a boring, everyday—"

She shoved him away. He laughed and pulled her back. "Maybe. Maybe he needs some heartbreak first so that he realizes what he's got when he finally finds it."

"Much better," she said. "So, where's Ethan?"

"At Mom's." Donovan ran his hands down her, curved his palms over her rear and brought her close. "We have plenty of time to go back to your house for a while."

"Actually, I'd like to go tell him, if you don't mind." Excitement filled her to near bursting. "I'm going to be a mother. I'm kind of in a hurry to celebrate that. Actually, I'm in a big hurry. It's something I thought I'd never have the chance—" She swallowed.

His expression was one of total indulgence to her happiness. "We can go tell him right now."

"Do you think, since he calls Anne Mum, that maybe he'll be able to call me Mom?" she asked, worried. "I don't want to replace her, just add to what she's already given him. And I know we need to give him time to come to terms with it all first. Plus, it means another move for him—here, to this beautiful house—"

He laughed. "Slow down. Take a breath."

She inhaled shakily. "Okay. O-kay."

"All right. Anything else on that list of yours?"

"Probably lots, but for now? No."

He hooked an arm around her, and drew her back inside the house. "This place needs a lot of work."

"Of course it does. But then, anything that's worthwhile does. I love you, newsman."

"It's about time you said it."

"I've said it in my head so many times, I thought I already had."

They stopped in the middle of their future living room and kissed. "Don't ever stop," he said against her lips. "I'll never get tired of hearing it."

"I love you with all my heart." She would tell him that every day, for the rest of their lives. She would let herself be spontaneous. She would laugh and love and cherish.

They would have big family parties. She would be a full-fledged McCoy for the rest of her life.

"I'll learn how to cook," she said.

Donovan laughed then, and the house—her house—smiled, too.

* * * * *

*Fan favorite Leslie Kelly is bringing her readers
a fantasy so scandalous, we're calling it
FORBIDDEN!*

*Look for
PLAY WITH ME
Available February 2010
from Harlequin® Blaze™.*

"AREN'T YOU GOING TO SAY 'Fly me' or at least 'Welcome aboard'?"

Amanda Bauer didn't. The softly muttered word that actually came out of her mouth was a lot less welcoming. And had fewer letters. Four, to be exact.

The man shook his head and tsked. "Not exactly the friendly skies. Haven't caught the spirit yet this morning?"

"Make one more airline-slogan crack and you'll be walking to Chicago," she said.

He nodded once, then pushed his sunglasses onto the top of his tousled hair. The move revealed blue eyes that matched the sky above. And yeah. They were twinkling. Damn it.

"Understood. Just, uh, promise me you'll say 'Coffee, tea or me' at least once, okay? Please?"

Amanda tried to glare, but that twinkle sucked the

annoyance right out of her. She could only draw in a slow breath as he climbed into the plane. As she watched her passenger disappear into the small jet, she had to wonder about the trip she was about to take.

Coffee and tea they had, and he was welcome to them. But her? Well, she'd never even considered making a move on a customer before. Talk about unprofessional.

And yet…

Something inside her suddenly wanted to take a chance, to be a little outrageous.

How long since she had done indecent things—or decent ones, for that matter—with a sexy man? Not since before they'd thrown all their energies into expanding Clear-Blue Air, at the very least. She hadn't had time for a lunch date, much less the kind of lust-fest she'd enjoyed in her younger years. The kind that lasted for entire weekends and involved not leaving a bed except to grab the kind of sensuous food that could be smeared onto—and eaten off—someone else's hot, naked, sweat-tinged body.

She closed her eyes, her hand clenching tight on the railing. Her heart fluttered in her chest and she tried to make herself move. But she couldn't—not climbing up, but not backing away, either. Not physically, and not in her head.

Was she really considering this? God, she hadn't even looked at the stranger's left hand to make sure he was available. She had no idea if he was actually attracted to her or just an irrepressible flirt. Yet something inside was telling her to take a shot with this man.

It was crazy. Something she'd never considered. Yet right now, at this moment, she was definitely considering it. If he was available…could she do it? Seduce a stranger. Have an anonymous fling, like something out of a blue movie on late-night cable?

She didn't know. All she knew was that the flight to Chicago was a short one so she had to decide quickly. And as she put her foot on the bottom step and began to climb up, Amanda suddenly had to wonder if she was about to embark on the ride of her life.

HARLEQUIN *Presents*

Sold, bought, bargained for or bartered

He'll take his...

Bride on Approval

Whether there's a debt to be paid,
a will to be obeyed or a business
to be saved...she has no choice
but to say, "I do"!

PURE PRINCESS, BARTERED BRIDE
by *Caitlin Crews*
#2894

Available February 2010!

*It all started
with a few naughty books....*

As a member of the Red Tote Book Club,
Carol Snow has been studying works of
classic erotic literature...but Carol doesn't
believe in love...or marriage. It's going to take
another kind of classic—Charles Dickens's
A Christmas Carol—and a little otherworldly
persuasion to convince her to go after her
own sexily ever after.

Cuddle up with

Her Sexy Valentine

by STEPHANIE BOND

Available February 2010

Silhouette *Desire*

Money can't buy him love…
but it can get his foot in the door

He needed a wife…fast. And Texan Jeff Brand's
lovely new assistant would do just fine. After all,
the heat between him and Holly Lombard was
becoming impossible to resist. And a no-strings
marriage would certainly work for them both—
but will he be able to keep his feelings out of
this in-name-only union?

Find out in

MARRYING
THE LONE STAR
MAVERICK

by *USA TODAY* bestselling author
SARA ORWIG

Available in February

Always Powerful, Passionate and Provocative!

REQUEST YOUR FREE BOOKS!

2 FREE NOVELS PLUS 2 FREE GIFTS!

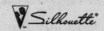

SPECIAL EDITION
Life, Love and Family!

YES! Please send me 2 FREE Silhouette® Special Edition® novels and my 2 FREE gifts (gifts are worth about $10). After receiving them, if I don't wish to receive any more books, I can return the shipping statement marked "cancel." If I don't cancel, I will receive 6 brand-new novels every month and be billed just $4.24 per book in the U.S. or $4.99 per book in Canada. That's a saving of 15% off the cover price! It's quite a bargain! Shipping and handling is just 50¢ per book in the U.S. and 75¢ per book in Canada.* I understand that accepting the 2 free books and gifts places me under no obligation to buy anything. I can always return a shipment and cancel at any time. Even if I never buy another book from Silhouette, the two free books and gifts are mine to keep forever.

235 SDN E4NC   335 SDN E4NN

Name	(PLEASE PRINT)	

Address		Apt. #

City	State/Prov.	Zip/Postal Code

Signature (if under 18, a parent or guardian must sign)

Mail to the Silhouette Reader Service:
IN U.S.A.: P.O. Box 1867, Buffalo, NY 14240-1867
IN CANADA: P.O. Box 609, Fort Erie, Ontario L2A 5X3

Not valid for current subscribers to Silhouette Special Edition books.

Want to try two free books from another line?
Call 1-800-873-8635 or visit www.morefreebooks.com.

* Terms and prices subject to change without notice. Prices do not include applicable taxes. N.Y. residents add applicable sales tax. Canadian residents will be charged applicable provincial taxes and GST. Offer not valid in Quebec. This offer is limited to one order per household. All orders subject to approval. Credit or debit balances in a customer's account(s) may be offset by any other outstanding balance owed by or to the customer. Please allow 4 to 6 weeks for delivery. Offer available while quantities last.

Your Privacy: Silhouette is committed to protecting your privacy. Our Privacy Policy is available online at www.eHarlequin.com or upon request from the Reader Service. From time to time we make our lists of customers available to reputable third parties who may have a product or service of interest to you. If you would prefer we not share your name and address, please check here. ☐

Help us get it right—We strive for accurate, respectful and relevant communications. To clarify or modify your communication preferences, visit us at www.ReaderService.com/consumerschoice.

HARLEQUIN
Ambassadors

Want to share your passion for reading Harlequin® Books?

Become a Harlequin Ambassador!

Harlequin Ambassadors are a group of passionate and well-connected readers who are willing to share their joy of reading Harlequin® books with family and friends.

You'll be sent all the tools you need to spark great conversation, including free books!

All we ask is that you share the romance with your friends and family!

You'll also be invited to have a say in new book ideas and exchange opinions with women just like you!

To see if you qualify* to be a Harlequin Ambassador, please visit www.HarlequinAmbassadors.com.

*Please note that not everyone who applies to be a Harlequin Ambassador will qualify. For more information please visit www.HarlequinAmbassadors.com.

Thank you for your participation.

BAP09BPA